11-02

Compression Scars

STORIES BY *Kellie Wells*

Compression Scars

The University of Georgia Press   *Athens & London*

Published by the University of Georgia Press
Athens, Georgia 30602
© 2002 by Kellie Wells
All rights reserved
Designed by Kathi Dailey Morgan
Set in 10 on 14 Electra by Bookcomp, Inc.
Printed and bound by Maple-Vail
The paper in this book meets the guidelines for
permanence and durability of the Committee on
Production Guidelines for Book Longevity of the
Council on Library Resources.

Printed in the United States of America
06 05 04 03 02 C 5 4 3 2 1

Library of Congress Cataloging-in-Publication Data
Wells, Kellie, 1962–
    Compression scars : stories / by Kellie Wells.
        p. cm.
    ISBN 0-8203-2431-0 (alk. paper)
    I. Title
    PS3623.E47 C66 2002
    813'.6—dc21   2002005542

British Library Cataloging-in-Publication Data available

For Joachim

and in memory of my mother,
Marjorie Ann Wells

Contents

I am indebted to Jaimy Gordon, Ellen Akins, and Catherine Gammon for their unwavering support, incisive editorial advice, intelligence, and friendship, and to the series editor, Charles East. I wish also to thank Stuart Dybek, Buddy Nordan, Nancy Zafris, Scott Heim, and Kent Nelson for their guidance and encouragement; Fred Wheaton for being my ideal audience; and Marty Lammon, David Muschell, and Sarah Gordon, whose supportive kindness and faith helped me to persevere. And a special thank you to my sister Jane.

"Blue Skin" was first published in *Columbia: A Magazine of Poetry and Prose*, "Godlight" in *Another Chicago Magazine*, "Stardogged Moon" in *The Gettysburg Review*, "A. Wonderland" in *Carolina Quarterly*, "Swallowing Angels Whole" in *Third Coast*, "Sherman and the Swan" in *Chelsea*, "Secession, XX" in the *Kenyon Review*, and "Hallie Out of This World" in *Prairie Schooner*.

The brief excerpt from Wallace Stevens's poem "The Auroras of Autumn," from the book of the same name, is reprinted by permission of the publisher, Random House. Passages from the writings of Aimee Semple McPherson are reprinted by permission of the International Church of the Foursquare Gospel.

Compression Scars

Compression Scars

The summer the bats came, Duncan began wearing only blue and my breasts grew a whole cup size as if I were feeding them better. The day I first noticed the bats, I had gone outside to watch the Roto-Rooter men dig up the Dorsetts' backyard. Mr. Dorsett paced back and forth as the muddy men lifted parts of the lame septic tank out of the hole. I admit I was sort of glad about it. I could tell the whole thing embarrassed Mr. Dorsett because he was stinking up the entire neighborhood. It was the end of May and even though it wasn't too hot yet, neighbors were shutting their doors and windows and turning on the AC.

Mr. Dorsett looked over at our yard periodically to see if my dad had come out to watch the cavern that Mr. D's backyard was becoming, and I'd wave and smile like we were old pals. Across Mr. Dorsett's yard, I saw Mrs. McCorkle. She was kneeling in her garden, tugging at something. When she looked up, Mr. Dorsett waved nervously at her, and she smiled and yelled, "Hello, Ivy." I smiled back.

No love is lost between Mr. Dorsett and me. When I was eight years old, he wouldn't allow his twelve-year-old daughter, Judy, to play with me anymore. He claimed he was afraid she would pick up infantile habits or her brain wouldn't be properly stimulated if she didn't hang out with kids her own age. Personally, I think he didn't like me because of my unorthodox religious views. I think he was just steamed because I told Judy that when I prayed, I said it to my stomach, because that's where I thought God was—on the inside somewhere, maybe swimming in my small intestine or spinning around in my pancreas.

Judy told me the next day she was poking herself in the stomach, on the lookout for signs of a higher power hiding inside her, when her father asked her what in Henry's name she was doing. Judy, a hopelessly brick-headed literalist, told Mr. Dorsett what I'd said and asked him if God in the pancreas portended problems for the body later on (having just covered insulin and bile production in science class). She saw divine diabetes in my future and probably pictured my organs sagging with the weight of being occupied so intimately. I think she was hoping to find the tumor of God inside her stomach so she could push him up into her arm or cheek or some other harmless spot where he'd be less likely to interfere with her bodily processes.

Mr. Dorsett was a deacon at a church where going to movies, even *The Million Dollar Duck*, was a sin, although it was A-OK to watch television. You weren't supposed to dance either. It was probably a sin if you were even caught swaying a little. And music was definitely out unless the lyrics mentioned rising from the grave or the blood of the lamb or something. I went to this church. Once. I sat between Judy and Mr. Dorsett. The minister didn't talk, he yelled, like we all had a hearing loss of some sort (after several Sundays of that, I think we would have—probably an evangelical strategy for quick, resistance-free supplication: deaf lambs don't bleat back, a way to shut the mutton up). He leaned out over the pulpit and practically screamed the Word. His face was puffy, and the thick folds of his cheeks filled with red. I don't think he got enough oxygen. He exhaled quite a bit, but I didn't see him inhale much. He had gray cowlicked hair that kept flying forward in an arc over his eyes. It's funny how some people think they have to look like they're having a stroke to convince you of the incontrovertible god's-honest truth of what they're saying. I remember shaking and kicking my feet during the sermon, and Mr. Dorsett slapped my knees.

So I was secretly pleased about this septic tank thing because I thought it definitely pointed to Mr. Dorsett's ailing karma. Actually, I am only a selective believer in karma. I believe in it when I think people are getting what they deserve, which, let's face it, is pretty rare. But I still have a hard time accepting the idea that hungry babies with bubbled, empty stomachs are in that predicament because they were maybe serial killers or jewel thieves in a previous life. Babies are blank, nearly smooth-brained, with a wrinkle for complacency, a wrinkle for fear, and a crevasse for hunger and thirst. So it's not like they'd learn a lesson or anything.

Anyhow, as I watched Mr. Dorsett pop Tums like they were Sweet Tarts, I saw them, I saw the bats. I didn't know what they were at first. I was picking a scabby fungus off our sycamore tree, half expecting it to bleed, and thinking it was odd the tree already had a few dead leaves. Then, a little higher up, I noticed these yellowish-brown bulbs, and it appeared our sycamore tree had suddenly grown peaches, like it was tired of simply being a sycamore and thought it might get more respect as a fruit-bearer.

I reached up to examine one of these dead leaves, and as I touched it, an electric feeling zipped up my arm and across my cheek. This leaf was soft and angry. It started shaking and screeching. I instinctively fell to the ground, in case it got the idea to dive bomb my head or something. It unfolded wings that were like little flannel rags, then it and a few friends dropped from the tree and flew off. As they screamed by, I actually glimpsed their faces, these furry little crumpled-up cartoon faces. They looked like one of those pictures you'd see in the backs of magazines or on the insides of matchbooks, and if you drew it and sent it in, somebody, somewhere, for a small fee, would tell you whether you should go to art school.

I examined the tree more closely and counted about fifteen bats total. Some were hanging freely on the branches convincingly miming dead leaves and others were curled up tight like tiny fists beneath real leaves. They ranged in color from yellowish to orangish brown, but none was black like bats are supposed to be. After I fully realized what I was looking at, I got a little spooked, thinking maybe they got their coloring from blood feasts. Then I noticed how beautiful they were. They looked like yellow flowers gone to seed. I reached up to touch one tucked beneath a leaf.

"You all right?"

My heart dropped into my Chuck Taylors. Mr. Dorsett. He scared the befreakinjesus out of me. You know how you're getting ready to touch something, maybe a smashed snake or an unidentifiable dark object lying in a corner, and some wiseacre comes out of nowhere and says something, or maybe your own stomach growls, and for a nanosecond you think the thing spoke to you, you think you just had a genuine brush with the godhead? Jeezoman, that's what I felt, until I heard the gate close.

"Ivy?"

"Hi, Mr. Dorsett." I brushed myself off and bent forward so my hair fell over my quadruply pierced ears, potential lecture fodder. "Too bad about your yard," I said. "Quite the terra carnage." I felt a thin smile spread across my face despite my best efforts to straighten my lips.

"What were you doing?"

"I wasn't dancing." I thought of that old joke about Baptists, who won't have sex standing up for fear it will be mistaken for dancing. Even though it had been eight years and Judy was now the sort of young Republican Type A personality urban professional overachiever I would never hang with anyway, I was still a little peeved at Mr. Dorsett. I didn't feel like being overly civil.

"What were you looking at?" Mr. Dorsett moved in closer and looked up at the tree.

"I was just looking to see, um . . . if that new tree food was working."

"New tree food?" Mr. Dorsett looked intently at my face, as if he couldn't believe his eyes, as if my nose had just fallen off and a big tulip had bloomed in its place.

"A couple of months ago, we got this revolutionary new botanical grow food they were selling on television. You know, it comes with Ginsu knives, or Popeil's Pocket Fisherman, I forget, if you order early. You sprinkle it around your tree and within a couple of months, you get fruit, apples or peaches, or sometimes even mangoes. Look." I pointed at the furry orange balls dangling from a high branch. Mr. Dorsett gave me this dour no-nonsense look like he'd had just about enough and if I didn't come clean soon, he was going to march me over to my parents and demand I be locked in the laundry room or shipped off to a reformatory for inveterate smart alecks or something, in the interest of the community.

"Bats," I relented. The way he dropped his jaw and began to back up, you'd think I'd said jackals or two-headed goats. "They're really neat."

Mr. Dorsett grabbed my shoulder and pulled me back from the tree. "Bats are dangerous," he said. "Disease-ridden."

"No, they're not." I didn't like how Mr. Dorsett was all nosy and pushing me around in my own yard. "They're little, harmless bats. They get bad press, but they're not actually going to morph into Barnabas Collins or Bela Lugosi for Christsakes." My heart raced as I said this last part—it came out of my mouth before I could put on the brakes—because I knew it was going to make the blood zoom in alarm to Mr. Dorsett's face.

"You listen here, missy . . ." Just then there was a minor explosion next door and black, foul-smelling goop started erupting from the hole in Mr. Dorsett's backyard.

"Looks like you got a gusher. Maybe you've struck black gold," I said as Mr. Dorsett raced out the gate.

*　*　*

I decided to go over to Duncan's to tell him about the bats. I knew he'd think it was totally gravy that we had bats hanging out in our sycamore tree. Duncan is my best friend. He moved to What Cheer from Medicine Lodge when we were both ten years old. The day after he moved in, he came over with two turtles, and he let me paint a red I for Ivy on the back of one. We tried to race them, but they kept going in opposite directions. Duncan said that was their secret strategy, that they whispered to one another, "Odds are better if we split up." Duncan and I have been inseparable ever since. Now, nearly every day, Duncan's father will ask, "You two attached at the hip?" And Duncan's mother will wrinkle her nose and say, "No, dear. They're attached at the heart," and then she'll wink. It's a little nauseating. Duncan's mom is super nice, but she can get on your nerves. She's the type that asks you every ten seconds if you're warm enough, cool enough, hungry, thirsty, etcetera, always on the lookout for ways to serve and placate. I think she took the gleefully self-denying good-girl lessons of the *Donna Reed Show* a little too much to heart when she was growing up. Once Duncan and I made signs that said, YES, WE'RE WARM ENOUGH. OUR BODY TEMPERATURES ARE HOLDING STEADY AT EXACTLY 98.6 and NO, WE'RE NOT HUNGRY. WE'RE FULL AS TICKS AND COULDN'T POSSIBLY EAT ANOTHER MORSEL. Mrs. Nicholson smiled and said, "Oh, you two," but she still asks.

Mr. Nicholson is a world-class cornball without equal. He's the kind of guy who steals little kids' noses, tells them that eating beets will put hair on their chests, as if that were a perk, and assigns them dippy nicknames that make them feel as though they're wearing their underwear outside their pants. Of course Ivy is an easy target. "That girl's poison, Duncan," he'll say. "You better hope you never get the itch for her." Yuk, yuk. When I was younger, he used to call me Intravenous de Milo, a nickname filched from *Spinal Tap*, which he'd been forced to watch countless times with Duncan, and he'd say, "I need a love transfusion, I.V." Then he'd make me kiss a vein. Once I said to him, "Boy, we'll never starve around here so long as you keep dishing that corn," and he quit razzing me, cold turkey, for days. I didn't say it with even a drop of malice, but I guess it took the fun out of it to have his behavior suddenly named like that, so now I just swallow it wholesale and roll my eyes like he likes. Mr. Nicholson calls their five-year-old neighbor Jill Shipley, Henrietta, for no good reason except that it makes her madder than hell.

If the caption WHAT'S WRONG WITH THIS PICTURE? were beneath a Nicholson family photo, you'd pick Duncan out in a second. Duncan has nappy, brown hair that curls off the top of his head like it's trying to escape. It's cut real short on the sides and there's a yin/yang symbol shaved against his scalp in the back. His favorite

thing to wear is a Zippy the Pinhead T-shirt that says, ALL LIFE'S
A BLUR OF REPUBLICANS AND MEAT.

Some of the beef-necked deltoids at school pick on Duncan.
They wear buttons that announce they are the FAG-BUSTER PA-
TROL. The insignia on the buttons is a limp wrist with a circle
and slash. They call Duncan fag-bait and say, "Bend over, Joy
Boy, I'll drive." And I say, "You realize the implications here are
much more damning for you." I whisper confidentially, "You're
obviously suffering from Small Penis Syndrome." Then I put my
finger on one of their big, clunky belt buckles, run it down the fly,
and say, "You really ought to have that looked at." Of course, they
shoot back, agile and witty as the redwoods they resemble, with,
"Stupid lesbo" or "Shut up, cunt." These guys listen to Guns
and Roses instructionally and dream of the day they'll bury their
girlfriends in the backyard. Real princes.

Duncan, on the other, less simian, hand, is beautiful, completely beautiful inside and out. His skin is white as Elmer's glue,
and if you look into his gray-green eyes too long, you'll slam your
foot down because you'll feel like you're falling. It's like having a
semi-lucid dream where you've just voluntarily stepped off a cliff,
and one of the things you're thinking about on the way down is
how they say you can have a heart attack if you let yourself splat
because you're *so* into it. But me, I always bounce. I'm into it too,
it's just that I believe in options. With Duncan, I know anything
is possible.

So about Duncan. After I watched Mr. Dorsett race around
the heaving hellmouth in his backyard for a while, I went to see
Duncan. Mrs. Nicholson answered the door, and she busted out
crying when she saw me. "I'm sorry, Ivy," she said. "Come in."
She hugged me hard and for a long time, like she'd just recovered
me from a kidnapper, ten years and forty thousand milk cartons
later. She pushed my hair behind my ears and cupped my face in
her hands. "You kids are so young," she said, and I could tell her

voice was only a few syllables away from giving out. "Duncan's in his room."

As I walked up the stairs, my mind raced, trying to compute the meaning of such a greeting. I became paranoid, which is my stock response to inexplicable distress in adults, followed closely by either blind self-blame or -defense, depending. I was worried that maybe Mr. Dorsett had told them he feared I'd joined a strange new cult, a druidic splinter group, that worshipped at the altar of tree-roosting bats. Mr. Dorsett tended to see rank-smelling theological peril everywhere he stepped.

But as I entered Duncan's room, I instantly forgot what it was I had just been stressing about, like some corrective, cosmic hand had reached into my head with one of those pink erasers and rubbed out those brain cells. Duncan was sitting on his bed reading *Death on the Installment Plan*, listening to Fad Gadget, a recent bargain-bin coup. *I choke on the gag, but I don't get the joke.* Somehow Duncan's skin seemed even paler, as if the glue had been watered down; his lips looked almost blue. "Hey, Dunc, what's up? Your mom's tripping."

Duncan stood up. "Look," he said, and started unbuttoning his jeans.

"Wow, is there some sort of planetary misalignment that's making people wig or what?" I made a feeble attempt to avert my eyes. I was in fact very curious about what kind of underwear Duncan wore—one of the few subjects we'd never covered. Striped boxers. Cool. He hiked his shorts up a little and pointed at his thigh, the scars from his moped accident. "I've seen your scars before. I like them. Except for this fading one on my cheek, I don't have any good scars." He turned around. The scars wound around his thigh and ran down his legs in widening, white lines past his knees. There were three lines that stopped at different places, as if they were racing. The lines were eerie, almost fluorescent against his milky legs. They looked like symbols or rebus, like they were trying

9

to tell us something, like maybe they'd spell out a message when they reached the appropriate point. Duncan put his jeans back on. "Jesus, Duncan. Your scars are growing. What's the skinny?"

"So much for swimsuit season," he said. He tried to smile. I hugged him. I hugged him like Mrs. N. had hugged me. Even though Duncan had put his jeans back on, I kept seeing those lines, as if a flashbulb had gone off and branded the image on my retinas. I saw the lines lift off his legs and circle around my head, curling in through one ear and out the other. I saw them slip under the surface of the skin in my face, making fleshy speed bumps across the pavement of my cheeks. I thought about the movie *Squirm* and the electrified worms that terrorized people, getting under their skin, literally. I wanted to make the droopy, gray crescents under Duncan's eyes go away.

"Hey, Dunc, remember that scene in *Squirm* when that woman turned on the shower and the worms started oozing out the holes in the shower head, and then she turned the faucets back off and the worms retreated?" I laughed.

"They think it's some bizarro thing called morphea, or sclero-derma, they're not sure. They looked at pictures in dusty books they hadn't cracked since medical school and scratched their chins, told me they were just nose and throat guys, not weird disease experts. But they think it's one of those one-in-a-million deals. Untreatable." Duncan pulled me toward him and kissed me. It was a desperate kiss, as if he thought it might have some therapeutic or medicinal benefit. His tongue went everywhere, touched everything, took complete inventory. I believe if he'd had more tongue, he would have kept going straight down to my esophagus, blazing a trail inside me.

I pushed him back. I wondered if this was one of his games. Sometimes Duncan is so childlike, almost obsessive-compulsive, a magical thinker. He makes up these games or rituals and con-vinces himself that his wish will come true if he completes his task. Like if he can successfully throw and catch his boomerang twenty times in a row while juggling cantaloupes, it's a sign he'll get accepted to UC Berkeley or receive manna, or something like that. The spooky thing is that it almost always works. I guess the psychologists would say it's just a self-fulfilling prophecy, but it's still kind of unsettling. I mean Duncan's no Nostradamus or Uri Geller or Tiresias or anything, he just knows what he wants.

"Morphea?" I said. "That sounds like science fiction. You're making this up?" I said hopefully. We sat down on his bed. I was starting to get seriously creeped out.

"No. I'm not."

"Is it some kind of sleeping sickness?"

"No. Misnomer."

"Spill it, Dunc-man. You're making me nervous."

Duncan fingered the shaved path of the yin/yang symbol shorn into his scalp. "I don't know if you remember the niggling details of my injury or not—who knew it was going to matter—but these scars I got aren't from being cut or anything like that, they're from the impact. You know, from being pressed up against the curb. They're called compression scars." Duncan stopped and looked at me like what he had just said was dangerously illuminating, the key to sudden understanding, and he was waiting for me to say a slow and knowing "Ohhh" and nod my head.

"Yeah, keep going."

"I guess we should have held out for more insurance money. Evidently these compression scars can come back to haunt you, big time. They can lie dormant like some goddamned ghost wound hibernating in your leg. And you don't know, you think you're fine. You just think you got some awesome scars to show the grandkids later on. Then these scars, they, like, come to life and spread across your whole body, and after they're done striping the outside, they can tear through your insides too, clipping the sharp

edges off your internal organs like goddamned scissors. Fuck."
Duncan bent over his wastepaper basket. "Maybe you ought to
go, Ive. I think I'm going to be sick. I don't have a stomach for
tragedy," he said.

"Wait. I don't believe this," I said. "I've never heard of anything like this before. This sounds like some made-up disease
from another planet, something you'd get inoculated for before
traveling to, I don't know, Neptune or something. Surely there've
been like a bazillion people who've had these compression scars,
right? I mean how come I've never heard of this?"

"I don't know, Ive, I guess it's not very high up on the re-
search priority list." Duncan wrapped his arms around himself.
"They just don't know shit about it. Fucking doctors. They're
not even willing to commit themselves to this diagnosis. You
could hear their malpractice-fearing knees knocking together every time they uttered the word *morphea*." Duncan began rocking
slowly back and forth on the bed.

I twisted the spirals of hair that hung over his forehead. "Why
didn't you tell me about this, about these scars?"

"Because. I didn't really know anything until today."

I felt my stomach start to knot in a way only a Boy Scout could
appreciate, hundreds of tiny hands pressing against the walls. "So
is it for sure . . ."

"Time to feed the worms? Should I prepare for the big dirt
nap?"

I nodded.

"They don't know. You could fill a thimble with what those
bastards know about it. They said it might stop spreading and
maybe it will never go inside. They said it could take a few months,
a few years, few decades, maybe never happen, maybe happen
tomorrow. Real conclusive stuff." Duncan looked straight into
my eyes and softened his voice to a whisper. "I'm afraid to move,"
he said. "It's like I have this big rip in my pants or something, and

if I move, I could die." He kept looking and looking at me, and I felt like he could see my thoughts, could see me thinking, *If you die, Duncan Nicholson, I'll, I'll cut off my hands and feet and sit in one place until I can come too.* His bottomless eyes. I steadied myself against the bed.

Duncan reached out and pressed his hand against my left breast, the larger one. "I don't want to die a virgin," he said.

I always thought this would be a great moment, that I'd feel velvety needles prickle against my skin. But it wasn't like that at all. It wasn't like anything. I couldn't feel it. If I hadn't seen his hand on my breast, I would never have known it was there. My breast felt novocained, heavy, but it definitely did not tingle, not a single goosebump, and I bump easy. I wanted to say, "Yes, Duncan. I love you, Duncan. Take me, take me," or whatever it is you say between hot gasps in moments such as these, moments that until this one I had only experienced vicariously through the lives of Chelsea Starling, secretly passionate nurse, and Vanessa Vandehorn, bored but sexy rich girl. But I couldn't. Had I wanted to, I couldn't even say something stupid like, "Could I please have a pretzel first?" My brain and mouth were momentarily disconnected. All I could do was stand up with my numb breast and dysfunctional lips and walk out.

Things can get so strange so fast.

*   *   *

The sun was going down and the cicadas were throbbing. I wondered if the sound bothered the bats, if it disturbed their sleep. I sat very still on the picnic table. I decided to keep an eye on these fraudulent leaves. My brain was still buzzing from the strange bomb Duncan had dropped. *Morphea.* It sounded like a name for a host of late night horror flicks—Morphea Bloodletter or something. I know I should have stayed with Duncan and tried to comfort him somehow, but I just had to bolt.

The bats were still snoozing. Mr. Dorsett still had a septic gorge in his backyard. I considered mentioning something about sky-tram rides across the smelly chasm next time I saw him, but decided against it. I guess I felt even Mr. Dorsett deserved a break. He was probably at church praying his head off, begging God to have mercy on his crummy plumbing.

I watched for signs of life from the wrinkled, brown leaves. You couldn't even see them breathe. I thought about their metabolism, how it must slow during sleep so they can preserve energy for flying and foraging. I imagined their lungs as delicate bubbles, filling only once or twice a minute, their button-sized hearts beating slow and steady as a bathroom sink drip.

I thought about Duncan, about Duncan before all this. I thought about the night we rode our bikes toward a storm. The lightning in the distance was constant and bright. We counted the seconds between lightning and thunder and stopped riding when the flash and bang were almost on top of each other. We parked our bikes and walked along a dirt road that sliced a huge field of corn in two. The air smelled hot, burnt, and my mouth tasted like metal. We stared silently at the lightning, appreciatively, like we were at a laser show. You didn't have to be looking in the right place to catch the silver zags either, because they were everywhere. And then I noticed the fireflies that hovered over the field, a blanket of yellow blinking above the corn in an uneven rhythm, a floating net of intermittent light, bright and fleeting stains against the black sky. I don't know how long I'd been holding my breath, but all of a sudden I started gasping. Duncan pulled me toward him. He widened my mouth with his hands, turned his head, and put his mouth on mine. I was surprised at how well we fit together, no overlap, better than clasped hands. Then he breathed. He just breathed. I wondered where his tongue was and what it was doing, but it was only air that passed between us.

My stomach burbled with the memory, and a strange feeling like lit fuses sparked and trailed from my nipples down to my thighs. I wished Duncan were here touching me. I was sure I would feel it.

The dead leaves began wagging. The bats were dropping off one by one and flying in an erratic, noisy mass above the tree. The sycamore suddenly appeared a lot healthier. Up in the air like that, the bats looked like jittery little birds. The streetlights snapped on. The bats flew over and circled the lights, swooping into the buzzing glow periodically, feeding on mesmerized moths and June bugs.

Then I heard screaming, and my first thought was, *Oh, no, they've gone and attached themselves to someone's carotid artery;* this was clearly the residue of Mr. Dorsett's repulsion. But it was Mrs. McCorkle. "What?" she yelled, as she moved slowly across her backyard toward the pit of tamed sewage in Mr. Dorsett's yard. She kneeled at the edge and looked in. "Harlan? Are you in there?" She wrestled a spidery vine out of the mud wall. "We'll have to clean this up. Mercy. Come on now," she said. She walked back to her house and disappeared through the back door.

Then I heard screaming again and things shattering. I walked around front and across Mr. Dorsett's meticulously groomed front lawn toward Mrs. McCorkle's. She was yelling at some invisible person, something about bluebells and pork roast, and smashing glass on her driveway. She lobbed an armful of plates and cups and jars onto the concrete and shook her fists in the air. She ran into her house and pulled her gauzy curtains off the rods. She ran back outside and started ripping them into thin strips. She spotted me at the end of her driveway and looked at me with narrowed eyes and tense lips, like she wanted to club me. My heart was pounding hard inside my chest, as though it wanted to get out before it was too late. I was 100 percent clueless as to a reasonable plan of action. I knew Mrs. McCorkle had these spells if she forgot to take some kind of medicine. I think she intentionally neglected to take it sometimes just because she was bored or lonely and needed her other self for company. Once last summer Mr. Dorsett was about to get into his car to leave for work when she ran over and started clobbering him over the head with a newspaper. She'd thought he was trying to steal her gladiolas. I admit I thought it was sort of amusing at the time, but now it felt like the whole world had completely kooked out, schizoid squared, like the planet had wobbled clean off its axis, and it was beginning to spook me but good. I wondered if some unstable isotope had been released into the atmosphere of What Cheer, or some volatile chemical that could take a once uneventful existence and turn it into something Lon Chaney would surely star in if her were alive (something Morphea Bloodletter would introduce on the Late-night Creature Feature). Or maybe the magnetic field reversal was finally here. Life, as I had known it, was out of whack.

"You," Mrs. McCorkle said, still sneering at me. "You. Where's Harlan? What have you done with him?"

"He's at Medicalodge South, Mrs. McCorkle, the nursing home. Remember? He's been there for a couple of months." I stretched my arm out toward her for reasons I can't begin to understand. I think the only reason she would have taken it would have been to rip it out of its socket and beat me about the head with it. Mrs. McCorkle snorted a few chuckles and ran inside. When she came back out, she had a large ceramic vase and a wall mirror. I backed up into the street. Mrs. Mc-Corkle threw the vase and mirror onto the pile of shards. The crash was loud and sounded final; glinting splinters of mirror shot across the pavement like sharp bullets of light. She smiled and kicked off her shoes. She raised her dress above her knees, and I could feel my panicked stomach trying to push free of my body. "Don't!"

She hopped onto the sharp rubble and pranced around like she was stomping grapes, smiling and stomping, dress in hand, as though she were just entertaining a tour group with this quaint, old-world custom. Then she went down on her hands and knees.

I think I may have screamed, but I couldn't hear it. I walked unsteadily toward Mrs. McCorkle, my legs springy like pogo sticks. I made myself think, willed thoughts outside this scene to come into my head. I thought of the bats, wondered if they were watching and if they were glad to be bats with their breezy lives, hanging in trees, eating easy meals, ignorant of the unseen perils of power plants, compressed skin, and old age. I would have traded places with them at that moment. I wanted to rise, lift up and out of this life, and would have given it all up—Duncan; my bootleg albums, the Soft Boys, Captain Beefheart, the good old noisy collectible stuff strategically swapped for at used records stores; the archive of articles I'd been compiling since I was a kid on UFO sightings and the Viking Voyager expedition; my memory of Grandpa Engel and his magical teeth; my face, my breasts—the whole shmear. Would have given it up in the beat of a tiny wing.

Maintain, I told myself. I made my way slowly to Mrs. McCorkle. I grabbed her off the razory debris and wrestled her to the ground, which was no easy feat. Those age-worn arms and legs held surprising strength. Crimany. At first I was afraid if I handled her too rough, I might crack her bones or something, and then I was afraid she might crack mine.

I finally wore her down and began picking the spurs of glass from her hands and feet. She held her hands up and smiled like a child who's made a mess of herself with spaghetti or ice cream. She looked pleased that we were both now covered in blood. Mr. Myers, next door on the other side, finally came out to investigate the commotion, and when he saw the blood and shattered glass, he started running around the yard screaming, "Oh, my god! Oh, god! Oh my god, Effie!" He picked Mrs. McCorkle up. She was playing itsy-bitsy spider on her shredded fingers. I could tell she was miffed when he made her lose her place. He carried her inside his house. My stomach finally made its way up into my throat, and I spit bile into the bloody grass.

I wished the bats would swoop down and pick me up by the collar and carry me off to some cold, quiet cave and feed me flies.

*   *   *

Duncan came over the next night and apologized like mad for being so pushy and forward and unromantic and all. He said the uncertainty of his body's future gave all things nascent and physical a kind of guerrilla urgency. It made me feel crummy because I thought I should be the sorry one. I mean, I was the one who had abandoned him in his moment of need. It wasn't like my sense of propriety had been wounded or anything. I think I just went concrete at that moment; maybe I was scared his skin might start falling off if we did it, like that grisly film of the aftermath in Hiroshima they made us watch in sixth grade. The captured shadows branded onto walls, the charred bodies, and all those people in the hospitals. And they just filmed it like it didn't even matter that the people whose bombed bodies they were documenting were completely raw, almost jellied; they just let the cameras roll. I always wondered what those cameramen had eaten that day, pears or sweet rolls, rice cakes, carrots, whatever, and if they had been able to keep it down. What did they do when they were finished shooting that evening? Did they take a bath? Did they touch themselves? Did they stare at their skin in the mirror, waiting for it to move? Needless to say, this is not an association you want to make just before your premier sexual experience.

"I think you're going to live through this, Duncan," I told him. "In fact, I'm sure of it."

"Yeah, what makes you so sure?"

"Well, last night I had this dream that we were old, ninety-five if we were a day, and we were sitting in a porch swing attached to this tree that I'm sure didn't have nearly as many rings as we had wrinkles, and 'Take the Skinheads Bowling' was playing in the background. We were talking about the concert we went to last week like it was the good old days. And then we started comparing scars. We both had scars all over our pruney bodies. I had a cool fish-shaped one across my stomach. You were impressed."

Duncan laughed. "At night I see my scars in my mind, and I watch them disappear as if someone had pulled up the plastic sheet on a Magic Slate."

I noticed that Duncan was clad head-to-toe in blue. Usually he wore ten or twelve competing bright colors, and you could only look at him for so long before things started vibrating, visually speaking. But today he had on a navy blue bowling shirt that said "Earl" on the pocket, blue jeans, blue Converse high tops, and a blue bandanna around his ankle; a small blue marble dangled from his ear. "Say, what's with this color-me-blue look?" I asked.

"It's chromatherapy," he said. "I saw it on Oprah or Sally Jessy, something. Different colors have certain effects on you emotionally and physically. Red is a stimulant. If you surrounded yourself with red, you'd constantly be doing chin-ups or something. Blue is supposed to be healing." He shrugged his shoulders.

That's one of my favorite-favorite things about Duncan, how he gives anything or anyone a chance. He accepts without complaint the absurdity that's as prevalent as ether and knows anything is possible, even good weird things.

I told him about the bats and about Mrs. McCorkle. Duncan loved Mrs. McCorkle because she always said outrageous things even when she *remembered* to take her medication. Once she told us if she were president, she'd impose capital punishment only for excessive chatter in movie theaters. "That would rid society of an insidious element," she said, "*and* help defray the population explosion." I think she meant it too. Duncan wanted to send her blueberries and morning glories.

I showed Duncan the bats. They were resting again, the withered foliage shtick.

"Are you sure they're bats?" Duncan asked. I pointed to the peaches near the top and showed him the ones clenched tight under leaves. "Wow," he said. "They're so beautiful. They look ancient and sacred. Like something in cave paintings." Duncan's voice began to crack. He gently placed both his hands on my breasts. "Do something for me," he whispered.

My breasts were tingling, hot-wired, bubbling with current. "All right," I said.

"What do these bats eat?"

"Insects mostly."

"What time do they start feeding?"

"I don't know. Around sundown." I began to wonder what it was I was going to end up agreeing to do. I had a feeling it wasn't what I had thought it was.

"Green and yellow are good colors, too," he said. "Restorative. I'll be back," he said, walking away. He turned around. "Tomorrow night."

*   *   *

When Duncan showed up, he was wearing only a busy madras pair of Bermuda shorts—no shirt, no shoes, nothing else. I hoped his scars wouldn't glow in the dark. He was carrying a jar full of blinking fireflies and a coffee can full of dead bugs. "Will you humor me, Ive?" he asked.

"This isn't going to involve like chicken blood, is it?"

Duncan smiled and shook his head. "What are your 'rents doing?" Duncan had this very serious look on his face; he looked sort of like Spencer Tracy in *Guess Who's Coming to Dinner*, like he was getting ready to make an eloquent speech on a touchy issue.

"I don't know. Watching a miniseries or something."

"Will they come outside for any reason?" Duncan grabbed my arm like he wanted me to think before I answered.

"Not likely. Unless the couch catches fire."

"Good. What about the Dorsetts?" He nodded his head toward their house.

"I haven't seen them. I think maybe they left town."

"Cool," he said. "Where are the bats?"

I pointed to the streetlight; a dark halo circled around it. "A couple stick around the tree and dive at the porch light occasionally."

Duncan took hold of my shoulders and led me under the canopy of the tree. He raised my arms and pulled my T-shirt over my head.

"Couldn't we at least use a tent or something?" I asked. For most things you can count me in; my name and the word *trooper* come up a lot in the same sentence, but an exhibitionist I'm not. I don't even like to undress in front of a mirror.

Duncan spread my shirt on the grass, pushed me down to my knees, then lowered me gently to the ground with my head in his hand, as if he were baptizing me. Out of the corner of my eye, I saw a bat dive into the light. Duncan took the dead insects out of the coffee can and arranged them on my stomach: a June bug, a cricket, some flies and moths.

"Duncan, you know, this is weird."

"I know," he said.

"I refuse to eat them, if that's what you had in mind." My stomach itched, but I was afraid to scratch, like any movement might activate the insects and make them bore into my navel or something, as if Duncan had preprogrammed them. Stepford bugs.

21

"You don't have to eat them," he said.

I was relieved. Around Duncan I do things that under any other circumstances would lead me to believe I'm certifiably off my noodle.

Duncan sat down next to me. He took some fireflies out of the jar, held them between his fingers, waited for the blink, and crossed himself, smearing the phosphorescent abdomens onto his chest. He lay back. Duncan scissored his arms and legs like he was making snow angels, only I guess they were actually earth angels, invisible. "Close your eyes," he said, "and do like I'm doing." I flapped and kicked, and it felt sort of nice, like I was a low-flying, upside down bird.

I felt something brush against my stomach. My skin was sparking, crackling with heat. I felt my stomach and my heart lift out of my body, finally striking out on their own. My legs shook. I let myself feel it.

Blue Skin

Clancy is watching the Oprah Winfrey show. There is a woman on who insists that the male Y chromosome is directly responsible for war and high interest rates. Her lips quiver as she speaks and she shakes clenched, white-knuckled fists at the ceiling. Her gums are completely visible.

Clancy prefers the straightforward sensationalism and sleaze of the Geraldo Rivera show. He especially likes it when Geraldo gets down on bended knee and squeezes the thigh of the sobbing guest. Yesterday on the show, there was a man whose wife had been slain by a woman driven mad by infertility. Despite modern medical advances, this woman could not have a child of her own, so she stalked a pregnant woman, kidnapped her and her unborn fetus, slit her down the middle like a melon, and stole the baby from her womb. The no-longer-pregnant woman clung to a tree as blood slipped from her. Some man out for a walk saw the dying woman, and he leaned close to her lips so she could tell him this story.

Clancy imagines his family will one day be the focus of a special edition of the Geraldo Rivera show. He can picture Geraldo looking intently into his eyes, caressing his knee.

Clancy grew up watching game shows and cartoons: *The Joker's Wild, Match Game '79, Rocky and Bullwinkle, Tennessee Tuxedo.* He remembers a particular afternoon when he was nine years old and his all-time favorite cartoon was on again. He sat on the floor directly in front of the television set while in another room, behind a door, his mother and a man spoke in squeaky, muffled tones, sounding like muted trumpets. On the television, a cartoon frog sang, *Hello my baby, hello my honey, hello my ragtime gal,* in an imitation of Al Jolson as he danced, straw hat in hand, across a tin box.

Clancy remembers tapping on his knee with a plastic hammer and kicking his leg in the air. He tapped up and down his legs and began hitting harder. He chipped away at his shins like a geologist freeing a fossil. He dropped the hammer and ground his fists into his calves. He bent forward and bit his feet.

Clancy's mother, Melba, emerged from the bedroom with strands of hair fraying around her face. She rushed up behind Clancy, dropped to her knees, and wrapped arms mottled blue and yellow around him. She grabbed his tiny fists.

"Your arms are colors," Clancy said. "Sky colors."

She cupped her body around Clancy's and rocked back and forth.

Somewhere in the house a door slammed, and Clancy broke

from Melba's embrace, fell on his side. Melba began massaging his legs. "It's okay now," she said. "The colors will disappear."

Clancy sat up. "No," he said. He looked his mother in the eyes. "My name used to be Clancy." He turned toward the television.

"What is it now?" Melba rested her chin on his shoulder.

"Clem Cadiddlehopper," he said, staring at the television.

Melba wrapped her arms around Clancy again. He traced the bruises on her forearms with his finger. "I'll always love you, Clancy," she said. "But I won't always be here."

On the television, a man grinned and held his hat. The man's forehead looked like a lawn sprinkler as sweat jumped off it in streams. The man picked up the limp and malleable frog by the scruff of the neck. He sat him on the back of his hand. He puppeted the frog along the box, kicking and dancing his frog legs with his fingers. The man let go of the frog, which slid off his hand in a heap. The frog ribbited indifferently.

"Neither will I," Clancy said.

*   *   *

It is evening and Clancy is at the Rosebud Bar and Grill. A charred sled hangs on the wall behind him. His band, Leopold and the Frontal Loebs, has just played. They covered songs by Joy Division, Roxy Music, Kurt Weill, the Velvet Underground, and Patsy Cline. A few people on the dance floor slammed into one another nonchalantly and there was some halfhearted stage-diving but little or no bloodshed. Clancy stands straight and still at the bar and feels house music throb beneath his feet. The layers of rhythm make him blink and swallow in time. He is only nineteen and not inflexible, but he prefers the simpler eras and droning dirges of death and glitter rock.

A tall, emaciated woman has sidled silently up to Clancy. She appears apparition-like before him, anemic and tired. She is clad in all black and is so thin that her face and long white hair seem fleeting. Her skin is nearly translucent, like the invisibly scaled body of a neon tetra. Her veins and blood vessels create a pattern like shattered ice beneath her thin skin.

"Pretty solid tonight," she says. Her wet, red lips look like two pieces of hot candy.

"Thanks," Clancy says. When he hears the word *solid*, it occurs to him that her appearance is that of gelatin, viscous and mutable. A test tube of glassy ichor ambivalent about the state of thickening, liquid stalled on its way to becoming solid. He recalls Mrs. Shepherd's fifth-grade science class. "The body is 83 percent water," she had said, her smoky, coffee-soured breath warming his neck.

"My pad?" The woman's voice pricks his ears. He shrugs his shoulders and follows her out. The bouncer grabs Clancy's face as he's about to pass through the entrance. He slaps it twice and pinches Clancy's cheek. "Can I see your I.D.?" he asks then laughs and pushes him out the doorway.

*   *   *

"So, are you Leopold?" The woman and Clancy sit at opposite ends of a turquoise vinyl couch with six perfectly square cushions.

"No."

"Who's Leopold?"

"He's a smart guy who killed someone just to see if he could get away with it." Clancy feels his heart thumping hard, palpitating in his chest, as though it were trying to reposition itself, get his attention.

The woman smiles and kicks off her shoes. "Friend of yours?"

"No," he says.

"So what's your name? Johnny Sinew? Dash Riprock?"

"Clancy." He takes off his glasses. Things blur and his heartbeat slows. He runs his fingers through a cowlicked spew of brown hair.

"Clancy? That sounds like a clown's name." The woman moves onto the cushion next to Clancy and pulls her legs under her.

"It was. It was the name of a guy my mom knew in Florida. He went to clown college there." Clancy begins focusing on small molecules of light that swim through his gaze, protozoan distractions.

"Wow. Vuja de. Synchrofuckinicity, hunh?" The woman laughs, puts her hand on Clancy's neck, and squeezes. "I didn't even know you could go to college for that. Pass/Fail?"

Clancy reaches behind his neck and brings her hand over his head. He shakes it. "Charmed," he says, staring at her hand, at the small, green lizard tattoo that appears to dart with every flick of her wrist.

"Yeah, right," she says. She notices Clancy staring at the tattoo and says, "Green is the most painful. Ow." The woman stands up. "I have an eating disorder, but I'm getting counseling." She puts her hands on her hips and swivels. "Do you think I'm overweight?"

Clancy shakes his head. She raises her eyebrows and leans forward as if to ask *No what?*

"No, *ma'am*," Clancy says. "If you stuck your tongue out, you'd look like a zipper."

The woman does not laugh. She nods her head vaguely and says, "Thank you." She grabs Clancy's wrists and turns them over. "No scars," she says. "You could almost have been a girl, you know? You have slender fingers and you move slow like you're just an instant replay of something."

"If you stuck your tongue out, you'd look like a zipper."

The woman smiles and sits. She scoots close to Clancy, leans over and licks his cheek. "Mmm. No stubble," she says. "Do you want to fuck?" She moves his shirt up and puts her finger in his navel.

"No," he says.

"Didn't think so. You're an insy." She begins to maneuver her fingers beneath his jeans. He grabs her wrist. "You do have a cock, don't you?"

"I have a cock."

"Just not led around by it?"

"Blind leading the blind," Clancy says.

The woman runs her fingers along the white, T-patch of scalp that glares through the closely shorn hair on the side of his head. "Why a cross?" she asks.

"A Saint Christopher's medal costs twice as much."

"You Catholic?"

"Just cautious."

The woman gets up and walks into the kitchen. Clancy puts his glasses back on. He notices a copy of *National Geographic* lying on the lacquered, petrified-wood coffee table. On the cover there is an aerial shot of a spotty rainforest with an inset of its native inhabitants. They have long, black and gray hair and weatherworn faces deeply incised with dark furrows, like relief maps made of leather. Round plates thrust their lower lips forward pleadingly, as if asking to be filled with food, answers.

Clancy traces the Indian's lips with his finger. "We're destroying the earth's lungs," he says quietly. He imagines pink, honeycombed membrane darkening, darkening. "We are our own cancer."

"I don't smoke," the woman calls from the kitchen. "I only put sugarless Sorbee hard candies in my ashtrays." She returns carrying a bowl of bean dip and a bag of pork rinds. She sits on the couch and says, "You know, you should really do more Joy Division covers. I could so get into a good Ian Curtis imitation."

Clancy feels his heart begin to knock against his chest again. "He killed himself," he says.

"Yeah," she says, smiling dreamily at the bean dip.

Clancy stands up. "Gotta go," he says. "See ya."

The woman raises one side of her shirt, exposing a breast as small and fragile as a teacup.

"Sure," she says.

*   *   *

Clancy thinks his younger sister, Willa, resembles her name: delicate and windblown, though she's actually quite sturdy. Clancy once watched as her black patent leather shoe met the step toe to edge and she fell backward down a flight of wooden stairs. She had on a ruffled, white dress and looked like a pressed carnation spread out on the floor. She picked herself up and walked back up the stairs, patting the banister gently, saying, "Nice stairs," as though they were a horse that had just bucked her. She never screamed, and she didn't bleed. She eats a lot of fruit.

Clancy teases Willa about the amount of fruit she consumes. It seems strange to him that a ten-year-old child would voluntarily choose apples over Ho-Hos. Yesterday Willa ate three peaches in a single sitting, and Clancy said, "Crimany, Willa. You think those things grow on trees?" Willa kicked him as she reached for a banana.

Clancy and Willa live with their stepfather, Buddy. Eight months ago their mother disappeared. She just didn't come home from work one morning. She worked graveyard at a convenience store called Gitty-Up-and-Go. Her purse was found lying in the parking lot of a Denny's in Kansas City, Missouri. Her keys, billfold, lucky squirrel's foot, and sunglasses were still in it, and there were two ticket stubs from the American Royal and a half-eaten Cherry Mash. In her billfold there were three five-dollar bills, two Susan B. Anthony silver dollars, a newspaper clipping about a child born allergic to her own skin, and the paper picture that came with the wallet of a grinning family of four.

Clancy and Willa and Buddy were invited to appear on *Unsolved Mysteries*. They ate lunch with Robert Stack and the television crew at the Denny's where Melba's purse had been found. The producer of the show—a tall, thin man with sculpted muttonchops and two front teeth a greenish white that didn't match the rest—asked Clancy to tell him everything he could think of that might be revealing.

Clancy leaned close to the producer's ear and spoke in a confidential tone. "Once, when we were painting Easter eggs, she told me there were people who lived in the Appalachians who had light blue skin, the color of robin's eggs, as the result of inbreeding."

"Good. Excellent," the producer said. "Now we're getting somewhere."

"She said it admiringly," Clancy said, staring at the producer's teeth.

"Uh-hunh."

Buddy was the only one who was interviewed on camera. He began to sob and said, "Melba, honey, if you're out there watchin', darlin', please . . ." He lowered his face into his hands. "Cut," someone yelled. Buddy pulled out from under the divan a ceramic plaque that read WHEN THE SMOKE ALARM SOUNDS, DINNER'S READY. On it were four neatly divided lines of white powder, and Buddy rubbed some on his gums. He inhaled two of the lines through a tightly rolled dollar bill. "Shit fire," he said. "Robert Stack's in my living room. My living room in the middle of fucking Kansas, man." He squeezed his nose and sniffed. "Fuck that Judy Garland, man. She's dead as a doorknocker. I got Robert Stack."

"On the edge," one of the cameramen said. "Technically, we're on the *edge* of fucking Kansas."

The woman who portrayed Melba in the reenactment scenes gave Clancy an eight-by-ten glossy photograph of her and her agent's card in case he ever decided to pursue an acting career. "You got the jaw for it, lover," she said. "And those hands . . ."

She gave Willa a bag of tangerines, a Sea Monkey kit, and a kiss. "I'm going to plant one right there," she said, pointing to Willa's cheek. She scratched it with her fingernail, kissed the spot, then patted it down. "There. Maybe it'll grow."

Willa and Clancy watched as she left in a rented car. The car had two bumper stickers, one that said, WORLDS OF FUN, and another that said, IF TODAY WERE A FISH, I'D THROW IT BACK.

*   *   *

Now, two months later, Willa wants to activate the Sea Monkeys. "I think I'm ready," she says to Clancy.

"All we have to do is add water and presto, dancing brine."

"What if they don't wake up?"

Clancy looks at the animated pictures of Sea Monkeys on the package. One is grinning and waving and another is flexing its biceps. "It says here that they're developing heartier strains of Sea Monkeys all the time." Clancy knows they won't last long and wishes he hadn't said this. He knows Willa will name them and look for distinguishing characteristics. She will claim that one has green eyes and that one can sing. She will give them occupations. She will say, "If he were human, I think he'd make a fine math teacher."

"I don't think I know enough yet," Willa says. "What if they want to know where baby sea monkeys come from?"

Clancy pulls Willa's shirt up, presses his lips against her stomach, and blows raspberries into her skin. Willa laughs, then says, "I'm really too old for that now, you know. But you can do it if it makes you feel better."

Clancy and Willa decide to let the Sea Monkeys remain dormant a little longer so they will all have something to look forward to. "We'll give them nine months to get ready," Willa says.

Willa wants desperately to go to the Rosebud to watch Clancy play. "Please, please, please?"

"You wouldn't like it, Willa. People smoke a lot and wear spiked bracelets."

"A woman called today. She asked me if I was yours, and I said 'yes'."

"Good."

"She said she has an eating disorder but she's getting counseling. I told her I'd make her a banana cream pie if she came over, and she hung up."

"We can go to the river now," Clancy says.

*   *   *

At the river Clancy and Willa wait for land-roving catfish to appear on the banks. Clancy read about them in an issue of *Omni* magazine. These catfish have developed semiprehensile fins and tails and hardy lungs. They have been spotted perching in banyan and palmetto trees in southern Florida. They have also been seen meandering along the highways. Clancy told Willa about them and she wants to meet them, wants to ask them where they're going. Willa is certain they will migrate to Kansas. She believes they will be attracted, like the rats of Hamelin, to the soothing hum of tires against the woven metal of the ASB bridge, the "singing bridge." She feels certain they will become hypnotized by the incantatory song of rush hour traffic, the cars singing, *Hear me, here me, hear me, here me.*

Clancy pokes a long branch at unidentifiable objects bobbing in the murky water.

"Do you think they call this the Kaw because crows live here?" Willa asks.

"Maybe. Maybe it's the snoring sound the river makes late at night when the fish are sleeping."

"I bet that's it." Willa throws popcorn onto the water. Gray-green snouts surface and the popcorn disappears.

"The world according to gar," Clancy says.

"One of the catfish will surely want to take a walk," Willa says. "Maybe he saw Mama."

*   *   *

Clancy drops Willa off at home. They saw no ambling catfish. Clancy knows Willa is nervous and curious. She looks for things with which to connect. "My friend Emma Perkins has a Petunia Pig watch," she says. "I have a Petunia Pig watch." "Smitty, Mrs. Baumgartner's dog, has curly brown hair," she says. "I have curly brown hair." "The front of the Buick has two big eyes and a smile like me," she says. "Seek and ye shall find. Seek and ye shall find," she chants every night before bed, her prayer.

Clancy imagines she is calling the number that connects her with an endless, measured thump-thump—the number for Frankenstein's heartbeat. Clancy used to call it when he was a child, and he would listen to it for hours, willed the beat of his own heart to synchronize with the sound on the phone. He wanted to be present when the thumping began to slow. If Frankenstein ever expired, Clancy was going to be there to hear it. He imagines Willa listening to it at this very moment. "Frankenstein has a heartbeat," she is saying.

Clancy wishes he could take Willa to Bagnell Dam where the friendly, fat catfish swarm for the tourists, whose hands rain Corn-nuts and Milk Duds. He knows she would love the big paddleboat and the freestanding faucet of running water suspended magically in midair. He also knows she would be distressed by the glassed-in chickens that peck at toy pianos for a handful of mash. He knows he would buy her a glittery goldstone necklace, a pair of Minnetonka moccasins, and that she would look deeply into every face of every stranger.

Clancy is at the Pierson Park tower. He scales the tall fence despite the warning to KEEP OUT. The tower has been off limits for many years, ever since a little girl climbed it, unsupervised, and fell from the top. Clancy tries to imagine this tragedy, but he can only picture water balloons with Magic Marker faces bursting on the concrete below. Clancy climbs up the six stories and looks out over the city. He thinks he can see the blue and yellow lights of the Southwestern Bell building flickering on. He looks down and sees a girl climbing the fence. She waves at him. She treks up the tower stairs and stands next to Clancy.

"My name's Zooey," she says breathlessly.

"Clancy." Clancy's palms begin to itch.

"Too cool," the girl says. "In numerology Z's and O's are totally sacred, so like maybe I'm the Messiah." Zooey laughs. "Unless you know someone named Zozo."

Clancy shakes his head. "You must be the one," he says.

"Go Zooey, go girl, go Zooey." Zooey churns her hands in front of her as though she were shimmying inside a hula-hoop. "I'm sorry. Am I being too forward? My father says I have an obnoxious manner. You look kind of familiar."

"It's the hands," Clancy says, and turns his hands palms up for her inspection. He looks at her hands clenching the railing. She has the letters H-A-T-E written in blue ink on the fingers of her left hand and L-O-V-E on the fingers of her right.

"Do you go to Pierson?"

"No."

"Wherever you go, there you are," Zooey says. "Or is it wherever you are, there you go? I saw it on a coffee mug in Macy's."

"Can I put my hand on your breast?" Clancy finds himself asking. Zooey turns her head to one side, as though she's trying to discern words through a din. "To see if I can feel?" Clancy removes his glasses and puts them in his pocket.

"What do you mean?"

"I think I've lost the feeling in my hands," he says. Clancy's mouth begins to water and he spits over the railing. He lays his head down on his leaning arm.

Zooey takes his free hand and pets it with her thumb. She places his hand on her breast. It feels to Clancy like a knee or a hat or a bagel.

"Fuck," he says.

* * *

Clancy dreams of Melba. She sits in Willa's plastic pool. Her skin is translucent and blue. Under her skin she is filled with white liquid, like milk in a blue glass. She holds her thin arms out to Clancy. He walks toward the pool, careful to step around the chalk outlines of fish floating in the tall grass.

Clancy hears the telephone ring. Or is it wind chimes? he wonders. Or the pulse in his ear? The grass, the chalk outlines have disappeared. There is only the velvet black of the undersides of his eyelids. He opens his eyes. It is the telephone ringing. Clancy rises and walks into the living room. He feels a smooth, weighted dangle of genitals brush against his inner thighs like clay bell clappers. He hears the click and rumble of the answering machine. *Howdy*, says the machine.

"Melba?" Clancy says. "Mama?"

You've reached the home of Melba, Buddy, Clancy, and Willa, but we're not in it. Leave a message, and one of us will get back to you soon as we can. Oh, and if this is Sheldon, your parakeet's fine. He must eat three times his weight in seeds every day. Hulls everywhere. Wait for the beep.

"Hey, dudescicle. What's shakin'? The scenery is here, etcetera. Oh, by the way, fu-uck you-ou. In the words of the inimitable Frank Tovey: 'I choke on the gag, but I don't get the joke.' Hey Leopold, I don't give a righteous rat's ass if you don't have a prick. Really. Call me anyway. Ignite. Burst into flames."

Clancy takes the small cassette out of the machine. Buddy only recently turned the answering machine back on. Willa insisted he leave the old recorded message intact. She was convinced that if Melba ever called and heard her own words, she would be magically lured back to them by her former life at the other end of the phone line. Willa believed Melba would be transfixed by the sound of her own voice, that her mind would walk along the miles of underground cable until it reached their front door. Clancy puts the cassette in a shoebox on which Buddy has scrawled the words *Personal Effects*. Clancy cannot suffer the idea of Buddy having the last word concerning Melba. Using a pencil with an eraser in the shape of Fred Flintstone, Clancy inserts the word *Side*.

Clancy remembers the origin of the Fred Flintstone eraser. He remembers Willa clutching the eraser in her tight fist like a secret. She had gotten it at the Ice Capades, which featured the larger than life-sized versions of the Flintstones characters cavorting on ice skates. Fred fell down repeatedly, often taking his sidekick, Barney, with him. Wilma and Betty were graceful, with their big heads cocked to the side, and looked like sleek animals as their spotted dresses waved.

Melba knew one of the ticket sellers and got fifth-row seats on the bottom tier of Municipal Auditorium. Every now and then when the skaters came near, slicing to a stop, they could feel a spray of ice prickle against their cheeks. Once Bam-Bam leaned over the railing and shook the hand of the little boy in front of Willa. Willa shrank into her chair at the sight of the big, cushioned palm reaching out.

Suddenly the lights began to dim, and Dino swished to a halt, center rink. A voice announced that it was time to determine who the two lucky ticket holders were. The children with the winning tickets were going to ride on Dino's tail as he wound around the rink, looping and curving. The numbers were called, and Melba raised Willa up by the waist, shaking her in the air like propaganda. Clancy stood and pulled on his mother's sleeve. "No," he said. "She'll get hurt. Please."

Melba smiled and ignored the tug on her arm. Willa hung silent and limp. Dino picked up the first winner on the other side of the auditorium then swung around and backed up near Willa. An usher took Willa from Melba's arms and placed her on a cushioned indentation in Dino's tail. She placed Willa's arms around the stomach of the little boy in front of her, who held on to one of the pointed plates that ran down Dino's back and tail.

Clancy remembers thinking that the animated Dino didn't have armored plates running down his spine, that they must be there only so that small children can ride on his tail. Willa looked back over her shoulder as Dino's four legs skated away, the tip of his tail swatting the air behind him. The song "Dizzy" played over the speakers. Children clapped and bit the heels of their hands. They waved fluorescent pinwheels in the air.

Clancy saw Willa let go. He watched as her arms released the boy in front of her. As she tried to clap, she toppled backward off Dino's tail. She lay sprawled on the ice. All the people in the auditorium gasped "Oh" at the same time like a canned response. People dressed in white skated out and scooped Willa up off the ice like debris. They took her to an office where a sleepy medical student waited for just this sort of calamity. The medical student looked somewhat disappointed to discover that only Merthiolate and Band-Aids were called for but forced a smile as he handed her a kazoo and a Fred Flintstone eraser.

That night Clancy rubbed Willa's feet as Melba rocked her back and forth in her arms. They fed her mint chocolate chip ice cream and bright pink marshmallow rabbits. Clancy colored in Willa's toenails with her turquoise-blue Magic Marker as they watched *The Courtship of Eddie's Father* on television. Willa cried at the thought of the deportation of Mrs. Livingston, the Japanese housekeeper, who always spoke low and hushed like a humming child. "She's the one that makes things calm," Willa said.

Dry sobs bent Melba's body, and she kissed Willa's bruised knees and scabbed shins. Melba laid her head on Willa's knees and petted her thighs. "Your knees aren't speaking to me," Melba said. "I'm sorry, chicken," she said. "I'm sorry."

"It's only blue skin," Willa said, patting her mother's cheek.

*   *   *

Clancy rummages through the shoebox. He touches all the objects: crocheted gloves, a tarnished Eastern Star ring, photographs, a mermaid-shaped shoehorn, baby teeth, a gold-brocade coin purse. He looks at a picture of Melba. Her face is blurred into the landscape behind her. She clutches her arms. Her grayish skin seems too big for her, as though she were getting ready to shed. Clancy sets the photograph down and slips his hands into the stretchy gloves, taut as new skin. He walks outside and digs a hole in the dry soil. He places Melba's picture in the hollow and tamps the earth down over it.

Back inside, Clancy clutches the Fred Flintstone eraser in his dirty, gloved hand as he walks to Willa's room. With blue chalk he draws the outline of a fish on her chalkboard. He sits down beside her and kisses her knees. Willa's eyes open. Clancy lays his head on her chest, listens. "And you have a heartbeat," he says.

Godlight

Jonas unscrews the burnt-out light bulb carefully, as though it were something he was going to plant and nurture, a tulip, an onion. This is what he does for a living. He works for the Hyatt Regency Hotel, and his sole occupation, the chore that fills his working days with purpose, is replacing darkened bulbs with sparking ones. He brings light. When a Sylvania soft-white reading bulb crackles its final current, it is Jonas who bears the replacement. He lights up itinerant salesmen's transient lives so they may distinguish brown socks from black; he brightens the shadowy corners of conventioneers' rooms so they may locate the wayward golf ball, the elusive shoehorn. He usually finds the owner of the spent light shaking it next to his ear like a quiet maraca. And Jonas, examining the gray bulb in the new light, will always say, "This bulb has lit better days."

When Jonas first began this job, he could not imagine he would be kept so busy. He was surprised at the constant rhythm, the death and renewal of illumination, like the cells of a giant body. Gradually he became skilled at coordinating the darkness so there were only isolated patches of confusion, stubbed toes. Jonas embarked on this career shortly after his daughter's disappearance five years ago.

It is Monday morning, and Jonas is in his own room on the thirty-first floor. He eats a bowl of cereal and watches the *Today Show*. He was saddened to see the female anchor, Jane Pauley, replaced. Something about the way she lifted her shoulders when she laughed reminded him of Carmen Miranda, for whom he has always carried a secret torch. He wishes it had been Bryant Gumbel who had been given the boot; he has written to Jane to tell her so.

Jonas is surrounded by many lamps and light fixtures, a gamut of bulbs. In the black and gold speckled art deco lamp with the loosely orbiting shade, there is the three-way bulb that blossoms from a timid forty watts into a glaring one-hundred. Suspended from the ceiling of his living room is a paper and bamboo lantern with its vertigo-inducing blue light. In one corner hangs a fluorescent bug light, clean as a baby's brain, having had little opportunity to stun and sizzle the brittle bodies of unsuspecting insects. Jonas keeps this one purely for show and comfort. He likes its silver glow and constant hum.

There is a knock on the door. Jonas lets in Dread, the bellhop. Dread is wearing his stiff green uniform with the black piping, gold epaulets, and brass buttons. Dread is pale as milk, and his jutting veins, tiny blue gopher trails, appear to be on the move and creep conspicuously beneath the thin skin of his throat. He has a pierced nostril, whose gold stud he removes during working hours. His head is buzzed to the scalp on one side, flanked on the other by a matted nest of black hair, which he tucks beneath his black cap. Customers frequently tip Dread well. Dread has told Jonas he believes they use him to alleviate their guilt over good fortune, motivated by the misconception that he's receiving chemotherapy. He is thin as a stick, but Dread admits this is fashion and effect, not destiny.

"Hey, Jonester man, I got something to show you." Dread begins unbuttoning his coat.

"This new gal just doesn't do it for me," Jonas says, gesturing toward the television.

"It's totally rad, man. You're going to freak." Dread removes his coat. He looks down at his chest and smiles. "Well, what do you think?" He begins flicking the tiny gold wires that loop through his red and swollen nipples.

"Doesn't it hurt?" Jonas touches a nipple gently with his index finger.

"A little bit, but that's not important. You know some guys get their penis or scrotum pierced to enhance sexual pleasure. There's this one guy I read about who actually had his penis split in two so he'd have double the sensation. Man, can you imagine? He does other shit like he wears a six-inch belt or sticks metal rods in himself all over the place. Wild shit, man." Dread licks his fingers and rubs his nipples. "Spiritual."

"I think all those things would hurt."

"No. He just psyches himself out, prepares himself so that the pain's expected and it's not pain anymore."

"I saw on a talk show where boys were hanging themselves while they masturbated. I can't understand that. Said a lot of them had asthma as kids. Something about longing for the paroxysm of not being able to breathe. Craziest thing I ever heard."

41

"That's a whole different trip, Jonas. That's called autoerotica and only weird fuckers dabble in that. You can fucking *kill* yourself doing that shit." Dread puts his coat back on.

Jonas stares at his hands. "I had asthma when I was a boy. It got so bad sometimes I just had to lie there stretched out in bed all day. I watched the neighbors' horses through my bedroom window. I watched how evenly they breathed and how their muscles moved along their bodies. I tried to breathe with them. They looked wet in the sunlight. And then in winter you could see the breath curling out of their big nostrils like smoke. I don't miss struggling to breathe, though."

"You masturbate, Jonas?"

Jonas looks at Dread and pauses before answering, looks at his shoes then back at Dread. "I did when I was younger. At fifty, seems kind of uncalled for."

"Did I tell you I found out I used to train bears in a circus?"

"What do you mean? Before you worked here?" Jonas raises one brow. "You're pulling my leg."

"No, Jonas, *way* before." Dread pauses. "In a past life. A previous incarnation? You know, Shirley MacLaine and all that. The transmigration of souls." Dread hooks his thumbs together and flaps his ascending hands. "Any living thing around you can be anyone who's not. Anyway, I hope I wasn't a bastard to those bears. I wish I'd been the tattooed man."

"You still could be."

"True. My future aspirations are as yet undetermined. New joke for you, Jonas. How many surrealists does it take to change a light bulb?"

"Surrealists? Hmm. I can't even venture a guess. How many surrealists does it take to change a light bulb?"

"A fish!" Dread snaps his fingers and smiles. "A fish, Jonas." Dread grins and walks over to the brass stand holding a covered cage. He lifts the quilted cover and looks under it. "Can I wake Thelonious up?"

"Let him sleep in," Jonas says. "He was up late last night watching the *Tonight Show* with me."

"Hey, Thelonious," Dread whispers. He drops the cover. "I got to go, Jonas, or Mr. Dickhead will be on my ass."

"You oughtn't to call Mr. Pritchard that, Dread. He's all right once the coffeepot's dry."

"Yeah, yeah. See you, Jonas."

* * *

Jonas watches television and waits for the calls that will tell him where the dark spots are. Next to his recliner is a TV tray with a can of V8 juice, a straight pin, and a telephone. Jonas is watching network television, but the commercials begin to disturb him; he switches to PBS. He is unnerved by how unashamedly cannibalistic some commercials seem. He has noticed lately how some advertisers will take a food product and make it cuddly and human. They turn the product, which is meant to be *eaten* after all, into something a child would love to sleep with if it were stuffed. You're asked to develop a sympathetic attachment to something you're later expected to stuff your gullet with.

There is a commercial for popcorn in which the kernels spend a day at the beach. They don sunglasses and douse themselves in suntan oil. One kernel instructs the others to turn on their stomachs, and then the sun's heat makes them explode. Jonas gasped out loud the first time he saw it. He actually rooted for the popcorn despite the demise he knew they'd meet. There are the commercials for StarKist tuna, in which the lovable but grade B tuna, Charlie, tries to hoodwink the fishermen into thinking he's really a prime catch so that he may have the privilege of being eaten under the StarKist label. "Don't worry," Jonas said glumly.

"Be happy. That's what they advise these days." And there are the claymation California Raisins whose rubber replicas can be purchased with a burger and fries. "See? Where would your careers be now if you had aspired only as high as a bowl of bran flakes?" Jonas said, shaking his finger at the television. Jonas regrets that children have to witness such misguided gluttony. He wonders if animal souls are also eligible for transmigration.

Jonas remembers an old commercial for Malt-O-Meal. The sales angle was that Malt-O-Meal sticks with you. It was winter, and a child who had eaten Malt-O-Meal for breakfast got bundled up to go sledding. As he walked out the door, he was followed by a levitating, steaming bowl of Malt-O-Meal. It followed him up and down the hill, trailing just behind the bobbing ball of his hat. Jonas thought it seemed menacing and would not allow his daughter to eat this hot cereal. He wonders if he should have fed her more hot meals.

Jonas sees his daughter's leaf-green eyes, her tiny nose no bigger than his thumb, her pink mouth showing through the holes in her white, knit ski mask. Emma is laughing and moving the holes to places where there is only skin.

Jonas takes the pin from the TV tray and pushes it into his scarred palm. He cannot feel it. He finds a less worn spot and sticks it with the pin. "I'm thinking about the pain in my hand," he says. "The pain in my hand. I'm thinking . . ."

*   *   *

Jonas's phone rings. "Hello?"

"There's a heat lamp out in the bathroom in 1516. Little girl called, and she's going to be there."

"Okey doke."

Jonas opens his walk-in closet. Heat lamps are stacked between the voluptuous mood-glo bulbs and the energy-pincher three-ways. In the basement of the hidden utility core, there is a closet filled with a bevy of assorted bulbs, but Jonas likes to keep the most requested stock on hand to save legwork. Jonas mistrusts elevators, sky trams, ski lifts, and cable cars. He has no faith in cable to carry him through. He was once stuck on a sky tram across the Royal Gorge. He sat with Emma, then eight, dangling over the craggy chasm. And he felt he was being toyed with. He had the unshakable feeling that he was a bauble, a trinket in the hands of some bored higher power, something to help pass endless time. "Do you believe in God, Emma?" he had asked.

"Yes, of course," she said.

"Is he a nice God, Emma?"

"He's very, very nice. He has curly yellow hair and shiny black skin and his name is Poodebaugh and he has a beagle dog named George. When I'm twenty-two, he is going to ask me out on a date."

They passed the time playing scissors, paper, stone, braiding each other's hair, and singing songs. They sang an echo song that Emma had learned in Vacation Bible School: *If you want to get to heaven, If you want to get to heaven, on a pair of skates, on a pair of skates, you'll roll right past, you'll roll right past, those pearly gates, those pearly gates . . .*

They had been stalled for nearly four hours when a woman in the car ahead of them began screaming. She crawled out of the car, and the man with her grabbed at her, pleaded with her to get back in. She crawled onto the roof and caught hold of the slightly swinging cable. When she slipped off the car, the screaming and the pleading stopped; there was no sound at all except for the distant crumbling of rocks.

Emma began shaking and twisting her skirt. "She'll get to spend the night at God's house tonight. She'll like it there. He has a very nice swimming pool with rainbow-colored water and a refrigerator with a spout in the door and if you push a button, it gives you chocolate cigarettes, and a pinball machine that you can't lose at."

❊   ❊   ❊

Jonas knocks on the door of room 1516. A young girl opens the door. "Hi, Chloe. Heard your heat lamp was on the fritz."

Chloe puts one hand on her hip and thrusts the opposite shoulder forward. She sucks in her cheeks, raises her eyebrows, narrows her eyes to slits. "Do they love me, Max?" she asks. "Who am I?" she whispers through tight lips.

"Why, you're Norma Desmond."

"Keep going," she whispers.

"You used to be big. You used to be in silent pictures."

"I am big," she says, "It's the pictures that got small." Chloe grabs Jonas's sleeve and pulls him in the room. "Do you believe in reincarnation, Jonas?"

"I can't say as I know much about it, Chloe."

"Dread says that we should all try to get people to believe in reincarnation because maybe if they thought they had to come back, they'd take better care of the planet this time around. Wouldn't it be awesome if I used to be Gloria Swanson?"

"I think it's awesome that you're Chloe," Jonas says.

"Boring, boring, boring. I have boring eyes, a boring nose, and *dreadfully* boring hair. The food I eat is boring, the shoes I wear are boring. My life is a snoozefest." Chloe rolls her eyes back and forth as though she were watching a tennis match on the ceiling.

"I think you're very interesting. I don't know anybody else your age who likes the old movies as much as you do, and I don't know anyone who has hair that is curlier or redder than yours."

"That is *not* a perk, Jonas. My mom calls it a mop. 'Go tame your mop, Glowworm,' she says. She's such a big b-word sometimes. I think she needs some romance in her life, don't you? She desperately needs s-e-x." Chloe throws herself across the bed.

"Hey, you're an eligible bachelor, aren't you? Not that it matters much to her."

Jonas shakes his head as he moves toward the bathroom. "Count me out of your scheming, Chloe. You watch too much *I Love Lucy*. Your mother would shoot me if she knew we were having this conversation. When's the house going to be done?" Jonas takes the heat bulb out of its bright red box and looks at the new packaging. Beneath the words *Dries, Warms, Soothes* stands a grinning woman with horns, a cape, fishnet stockings; she holds a pitchfork.

"Oh, who knows. It will probably melt from global warming or be sucked into the earth for being on top of an Indian burial ground before then anyway." Chloe sighs.

Jonas hands the bulb to Chloe. "You know, with moderate usage one of these has roughly the same average life span as a trumpeter swan."

"Wow, what a cool fact! You're the coolest old guy I know, Jonas. So how come you're not married? Got any kids?"

Jonas flips the switch in the bathroom. The old heat lamp buzzes on.

"So I lied. It's so dull down here, Jonas. Is it possible to die of boredom? Sometimes I think I'll go out of my gourd." Chloe crosses her eyes.

Jonas takes the bulb and puts it back in the box. "Well, come up and see me. You know I've got to stay put during the day for legit calls."

"Jeez Louise. It's noon. Can't they just open their curtains if they need light so bad?"

"Sometimes it's a call for a bathroom light or it could be a light out in one of the hallways or in the lobby or the kitchen." Jonas walks toward the door.

"Poop. I have to stay here in case any of the workmen call about the house. If they do, then I have to call Mom and tell her to call them back. She's really paranoid about them having her number at work. She thinks they'll call her every ten minutes just to bug her if they do. Like they've got nothing better to do than check in with her. She's such a solipsist."

Jonas raises his eyebrows. Chloe points to a book on the nightstand: *Thirty Days to a Bigger Vocabulary.* "At least if I have to talk to myself, I'll have intelligent conversations," Chloe says.

"You know what they say about solipsists, don't you?"

"Who?"

"In general."

"Oh, a joke. No. What do they say?"

"If you meet one, you better take good care of her since the world revolves 'round her." Jonas stifles his laugh as he waits for Chloe to respond. Chloe picks up the book and thumbs through it.

"Oh, I get it." Chloe smiles. "I'll have to remember that one. Did you get that from Dread? Hey, Jonas, you want to hear my all-time favorite joke?"

"Sure."

"Okay. This is an audience-participation joke. Twirl your finger in the air like this." Chloe circles her index finger as if she were spinning a plate on it. Jonas imitates the gesture and Chloe stops. "Okay, keep doing it. Knock, knock?"

"Who's there?"

"Ya."

"Ya who?"

Chloe laughs out loud and pounds her fists against the side of the bed. Jonas smiles and shakes his head. "You're a corker, Chlo."

"When I told that joke to Dread, he said I was a real cod. That's what he called me. I go for the easy laughs."

"I'll see you later, Chloe."

"See you, Jonas." Chloe walks out into the hall. "Guess this swan has a few more years left, hunh."

Two weeks before Emma disappeared, she showed Jonas a glow-in-the-dark superball. "It's a ghost's eyeball," she said. "If you hold it under the light then take it in the closet, it can see again."

"Where did you get it, Emma?" Jonas asked.

"Jesus."

"What?"

"Jesus gave it to me for being good and clean."

"Did you get it at Sunday school?"

Emma shook her head and rolled the ball between her hands.

"Where did you see Jesus?"

"At the park. He looks like the pictures except there weren't any thorns or light. He said he'd give me some Fruit Stripe gum next time."

"Oh, he did?" Jonas smiled and kissed Emma's nose.

Jonas finds himself remembering the park and the lilt of the swallowtail butterfly, the bobbing black and yellow, the last thing he saw Emma reach for before she disappeared behind bushes. Sometimes he cannot recall the details of Emma's face without the aid of a photograph, but the image of her tiny, reaching hands, tilted and cupped as though they were holding an invisible bowl, returns to him clearly again and again. In these memories, Emma's hands are always the same, though the atmosphere surrounding them changes: sometimes it is bright blue, a painted backdrop, and other times it is dark and shadowy and swallows her hands like a giant mouth, but occasionally the hands are backlit as if bearing a beatific secret. Jonas wishes he had held these hands more often. He stares at his own hard palms.

Jonas sets Thelonious on his shoulder. Thelonious is a Monk parakeet, a small breed of parrot. He is green as bluegrass with a striped gray breast and a tan beak. Jonas turns on the TV and presses buttons on the remote control until he finds *Newton's Apple.* A ten-banded armadillo in a large glass aquarium scratches at rocks.

"What are you doing?" Thelonious says. Thelonious begins to preen Jonas's hair.

"Just watching TV. What are *you* doing? Looking for grubs?"

"What are you doing. Hello. What are you doing. Go potty."

"Do you have to go potty?" Jonas grabs Thelonious, who chews at his knuckles. He perches Thelonious on his finger and holds him over some newspaper. "Go potty." Thelonious leans forward, trying to reach Jonas's shirt. He begins moving up Jonas's finger. Jonas holds up his thumb so he can't get past. "You brought it up, so go potty." Thelonious squats.

"Good bird." Jonas kisses Thelonious and sets him back on his shoulder. "I'll have to show Chloe that trick. I bet she'd get a big kick out of it." Thelonious resumes preening. He begins chewing on Jonas's ear. Jonas gently raps Thelonious on the beak. "That's no nit, Thelonious. Desist."

Armadillos are the only other mammals that can contract leprosy. A woman on the TV holds the armadillo up so the audience can see his soft underbelly.

"Wonder if armadillos in the pink of health exile the leper armadillos," Jonas says. "Maybe they make them stay on highway islands." Jonas laughs. Thelonious echoes his laugh. "Maybe armadillos have their own mythology, tell a story about an armadillo savior that raised a leper armadillo from the dead and miraculously cured his disease with a mere wag of his tail." Jonas laughs. Thelonious laughs.

The phone rings. "Hello," Thelonious says.

"Pipe down." Jonas picks up the phone. "Hello?"

"Yeah, Jonas. There's a lady in 2410 says her lamp keeps blinking on and off. Sounds like the type to be spooked by such things. Better check it out."

"Will do."

Jonas knocks on the door of 2410. A fair-skinned woman answers. She has tall, blue-black, ratted hair covered by a sheer scarf and thick, shiny, red lips; her eyes are hidden behind jeweled sunglasses. "Yes?" she asks in a gravelly whisper.

"You called about a persnickety lamp, ma'am?" Jonas smiles. The woman continually licks the corners of her mouth and clenches and relaxes her hands. The woman reminds Jonas of a wild cat, a leopard or a lynx, moody and tightly coiled. He feels as though he's on an accidental safari, his toolbox a tranquilizer gun.

The woman grabs Jonas by the hand carrying the toolbox and pulls him into her room. She closes the door behind him. "I'm Flora," she says. "Thank you for coming."

"Hear you got a lamp with a nervous tic." Jonas looks around the room for the guilty flicker.

"What's that supposed to mean?" Flora chews on her fingers.

"Just meant I'm here to fix your lamp." Jonas notices Flora's hands. She has long, sculpted, sharply steepled nails, but there are cuts, scabs, and freshly bloodied spots surrounding the cuticles.

Flora removes her sunglasses. The skin on her face seems taut, as though her hair were pulled back in a too-tight ponytail. "I suppose you're wondering why exactly I look the way I do."

Jonas shrugs his shoulders and shakes his head.

"Can you keep a secret, what's your name?"

"My name is Jonas."

"Jonas, you look like a decent soul, and I really need a complete stranger I can confide in. Would you please be that stranger for me, Jonas?" Flora takes Jonas's toolbox from his hand, sets it on the floor, and leads Jonas by the elbow to the bed. They sit down.

"Look, miss . . ."

"Shhh." Flora puts a finger to Jonas's lips. "No, please. Just listen. My real name isn't Flora and I'm not from around here. Actually, I'm just passing through on my way to . . . somewhere else. It's about the only place they won't look. I'm just here for some bridgework and some R and R to recover from the other reconstructive surgery." The woman begins to rub her cheeks.

"Miss Flora, I'm just here to fix your lamp, heard you had a flickering light." Jonas stands up.

Flora pulls him back down. "Well, you would too if you'd been through what I've been through. Look." Flora runs her finger along her jaw line, tracing a thin seam. It looks to Jonas as though her face has been sewn on, a tight mask. "I turned state's evidence on my murdering ex-husband and joined the witness protection program. They gave me a new face, new name, new hair, new everything. They said they could even give me new fingertips if I wanted. Wait. I'll show you. This is what I used to look like." Flora takes a billfold out of a purse. She removes a tattered picture that appears to have been cut out of a magazine. She hands it to Jonas. "I used to be some looker, hunh?"

Jonas recognizes the woman in the picture to be Rita Hayworth. She lies sprawled and twisting on a satin sheet, red hair wreathing her face. "Yes. You were awfully pretty," he says. Jonas stands up and turns on the light that sits on the nightstand.

"Don't," Flora screams. She pushes the lamp onto the floor. It snaps dark. "Out like a light." Flora bends over her knees and grabs her feet. Jonas sees her body shudder, but she is silent. "He killed my baby," she says, her face pressed between her shins. "Him and those doctors took her, and they snapped her head like she was a dandelion or a tiddlywink. They said it was empty. But I know she just wasn't done yet. She came early. But they wouldn't give her time. They said she was blind and deaf and couldn't even coo. They said she had only enough brain functioning to keep her barely alive. Said she was no more than a carrot or a potted plant. My beautiful little baby. My little premature baby." Flora stands up. She picks up the lamp. "Then they held her up to a bright light. They held her head next to the hot bulb so I could see it was empty. The light shined right through to the other side like it was only a little pink balloon." Flora strokes the round body of the lamp. "It's not the God-light we're *all* looking for, you know. It wasn't the Godlight. It didn't mean anything. It didn't give me peace or answers. They just didn't give her enough time. They wouldn't give her a chance to try harder." Flora sits on the floor and clutches the lamp.

Jonas bites into his lower lip, chews. He tastes blood, thinks about the stinging in his mouth, continues to chew.

*　　*　　*

Jonas sits in darkness in his room. He sings softly to himself. *The wonderful thing about tiggers, is tiggers are wonderful things. Their tops are made out of rubber, their bottoms are made out of spring.*

"Where are you Emma Dilemma? What are you seeing now? Is your God everything you'd hoped he would be?"

Our Father who art in heaven, Harold be thy name.

That's why it's Jesus H. Christ.

Jonas sees Emma's picture on the milk carton, the shadowy black-and-white picture. The police artist shows him the computer projection of what she will look like when she's thirteen. He wonders how the computer knows she will let her hair grow long. He knows it means nothing, but he is comforted nevertheless by the fact that she has no new facial scars and still has her front teeth. It is good she is still smiling, he thinks. He asks to see what she would look like if she lived to be twenty, if she is not already only a memory. They tell him to go home, eat some soup, sleep.

Jonas pushes the pin into his palm. He feels nothing but a slight pressure.

*   *   *

Jonas walks the streets downtown. He stares at the dirty neon and flashing lights. An arrow of yellow bulbs blinking on and off points to a pink neon sign that says RAY'S PLAYPEN. Further along there is a blue neon champagne glass effervescing three ascending circles beneath a red neon MILTON'S. The circles make Jonas think of Dread's flapping hands. A man stands under the sign. He has long blond hair and a reddish beard. He wears a Rolling Stones T-shirt, black with red lips and a long, lolling tongue. He reaches out to Jonas's arm as Jonas walks by. "I am the one," he says. "The good one. I will die for your sins for only five dollars. You can resurrect me personally for ten."

Jonas immediately spots the tracks reddening the man's forearm. The man leans forward and kisses Jonas's forehead. Jonas starts to walk away.

"Everybody's a goddamned Judas," the man says.

Jonas turns around. "Do you know where my daughter, my Emma, is?"

"Sure, man. She's safe. She's safe, man. Sleeping. Sleeping like a baby. Ain't no harm going to come to her. I'll see to that. She's happy. Real happy. Like a clam at high tide she is."

"What's your name? Is your name Harold?"

"Yeah, that's my name all right. My name's Harold." He moves toward Jonas. "I am the one. The one you heard about. I can show you the truth. Cheap." Harold's legs quiver and pulse, as though the earth were moving beneath only his feet.

Jonas takes out his billfold and hands Harold a ten-dollar bill.

Harold takes it, fixing his eyes on Jonas's. "Your place is set. All is forgiven. The kingdom is yours. Your daughter is happy. She's free. She's been set free, she's eating peaches. She'll be in touch. And I'll tell you something else, Jack. Something that means something. Knowledge." Harold leans toward Jonas. He breathes heavily in his ear and kisses it. He whispers, "We got tornadoes because we drive on the wrong side of the road, man.

54

Counterclockwise. Think about it. Only you can stop it." Harold turns and walks back toward Milton's.

*   *   *

Jonas looks out his window at the city awash in neon. He reads the newspaper as Thelonious paces his shoulder. "Hello," Thelonious says.

A man was found dead in the alley behind Milton's. Jonas knows it is Harold. *An unidentified male Caucasian in his mid-thirties was found dead. . . . Cause as yet uncertain. . . . Any information leading to his identity . . .* "What are you doing?" Thelonious asks.

Jonas imagines Emma and Harold together. They lie on their backs amid the thick stems of sunflowers. They puff on chocolate cigarettes and reach into the air. A tangle of green birds hovers above them as the light needles their faces. "They'll be back," Jonas says.

"Hello."

My Guardian, Claire

When I was six years old, a ring of shingles wound around my mother's waist like a belt, and she stopped breathing when the ends met. *Dr. Avery Schoenfeld's Bedside Guide to Good Health* says death by a girdle of shingles is a myth. It says it is a superstition dating back to the early Greeks. Evidently it is a myth in which my mother believed.

Claire took me in when disease cinched my mother's shrinking waist. Claire lived by myths of her own making.

I hope my mother felt no pain as the skin scabbed round her middle. I hope it was like slipping into a dream. She told me she had dreamt me, my birth. She said it was clean and pain-less. She was relieved I was a boy, she said, because boys depart from the mother, splinter from God, more quietly than girls. She said I dropped from a cloud, rain dark at the edges with my ex-pulsion, and tumbled down a shaft of wind, wet and silent as a mackerel.

Muddy-brown pin curls decoratively framed my mother's oval face. They were so perfectly circular, they made me dizzy if I looked at them too closely. They looked like they'd been scrib-bled on with a Busy Buzz Buzz. She had tiny hands that nearly disappeared when she closed them and three freckles in a row above her upper lip, like ellipses, like there was more to be said.

After the burial, I became Claire's full-time charge.

Claire was a beauty operator, which made me think she carved good looks from flawed faces with scalpel and suture, but it was hair she shaped. She worked out of her basement, where she had two pedestaled chairs bolted to the floor. Whenever Claire pumped the chair up so that the customer's head was at a work-able height, it made me think of Elmer Fudd and Bugs Bunny in the "Barber of Seville" cartoon. I imagined Claire perched on the heads of the customers, massaging hair oil into their scalps with all four paws. I saw wet-headed women careening toward the ceil-ing and bursting through Claire's roof. When I told Claire about my vision she said, "That Bugs Bunny. Whatever happened to him? A *huge* talent."

Claire wasn't like the adults I knew. People in the neighborhood and at the grocery store and the filling station called her "Claire the Loon." She said she was flattered. She loved birds.

Some people thought it a scandal that my mother had made Claire, no blood relation, my godmother. My mother respected a well-crafted pin curl. Claire was always very polite to her and brought her a brisket when our German shepherd was poisoned. My mother and Claire had the same sense of kindness.

Claire's daughter and husband drowned in a boating accident during a fishing trip five years before I went to live with her. The only thing she ever said to me about it was that it made her feel sad for stealing the worms from the robins that had worked so hard at unearthing them that morning. Once she told me she had phantom pains of maternity that made her bowels ache and that she missed the smell of aftershave on the pillowcase. Then she sucked on my toes and stroked my feet and fell asleep.

I was both surrogate spouse and child to Claire.

And I was sweet on her.

She gave me apples she'd picked herself. "They're not from my trees," she'd say, "but God doesn't mind and Johnny Appleseed is dead." And then she'd laugh, her eyes turning to tiny fists, the gap between her front teeth threatening to pull me in. Sometimes they were only crab apples, and we pitched them at cats when they stalked the birds, stealthing along near the shrubbery. Claire said they were called crab apples because if they could talk, they wouldn't have anything nice to say. Claire, my godmother, had spoken with angels.

They were sitting on her kitchen table, dangling their feet when she came in the back door. They smelled bad and had dirty knees and necks. One had white hair, a wrinkled face, and a crusted, runny nose; the other had red hair, red freckles, and wore silver high heels and white socks. They were both small and shifty, ungraspable as beads of quicksilver. They had eaten all Claire's sugar and vomited on the floor. They'd stayed to apologize.

I asked Claire how she knew they weren't just neighbor kids or ghosts. She said she recalled them from her time in heaven. She said as she was waiting to be born, they brought her a box of Good and Plenty and a bottle of grape Nehi with a crazy-curl straw. She remembered them. She said angels are as distinct as snowflakes.

That was when she first saw her father—in heaven. He had been in an airplane that was shot down over the Pacific Ocean exactly one month before Claire was born. He was entering the Kingdom just as Claire was departing. As they passed, he told her to help her mother with the daily chores when she was old enough and to act surprised the first time she saw a picture of him. She said he was thin and young and handsome and made her think of an antelope. When I asked her what her earliest memory was—and I asked her often, thinking it might change—she always grinned and clutched her elbows and told me about making her father's acquaintance in heaven.

Claire believed we carry with us prenatal knowledge that is mostly lost to us at that moment of induction, that first unencumbered pulse, that first slap into the material world. From that moment on, we forget and spend the rest of our lives trying to remember, grasping at dim and darting shadows of distant occurrences. Before we are born, though, we're tiny fibers coiled in a cosmic blanket that connects us with everything, a throw God covers himself with when he's chilled. Claire believed God dwelled on the inside. Inside all things. Inside the body like a benevolent growth, benign but swelling. She believed you could see God in the furrows of a peach pit if you looked hard enough.

And she believed in genetic memory. Claire said she was often surrounded by antiquated objects in her dreams, like buttonhooks or railroad lanterns, things that felt familiar but that she swore she'd never seen before, not even as a child, in a flea market, or on television. This belief was influenced, I think, by a newspaper article about a young boy who dug up a small fortune buried in the backyard of what turned out to have been an estate once owned by his great, great, great, great grandfather. Supposedly, this knowledge had been passed along genetically from generation to generation, like a pocket watch. It had slipped through the seed, through the blood, through the twisted cords of chromosome into this little boy's unsuspecting brain. Claire's conviction about this phenomenon was more hopeful than heartfelt, though she clung to her celestial recollections with the kind of tenacity that comes only from being touched by something pure and unimaginable, something beyond bald data and observable evidence—something no Freudian interpretation could tarnish.

One midnight in May when I was ten, Claire and I lay on our stomachs with the sides of our faces resting in the freshly tilled dirt, listening. I heard nothing.

"Silence," Claire said. She could sniff out skepticism at twenty paces. I was a new soul and so naturally incredulous she said. Silence was all that I heard.

After a while, I felt something, something infinitesimal burrowing in the ground beneath my cheek. I imagined it was a tiny organism invading the dwellings of sleeping nits. At this same moment, I heard a distant chorus of muffled wheezing that seemed to emanate from someplace deep and hollow. I thought this might be a trick of Claire's, like when I could tell she was moving the Ouija pointer. But the sound was too removed, too disembodied and eerily pitched to be Claire. Claire spread her arms and legs out and flapped and scissored them across the earth. She was making earth angels.

"I heard it, Claire," I said. We had just planted our garden by the flat light of the moon. On this night it looked more bilious than silvery, but it was in full bloom and Claire believed this was the best time to sow, because of the gravitational pull on the sap. She believed you could hear the inception of life if you listened closely enough, and Claire's ears were often to the ground. I believed she could hear the rustling of insect wings in Outer Mongolia if she tried.

*　*　*

Claire had a porcelain pallor. Her skin was that shade of white that was so white it almost glowed a moony green. The skin of her doughy thighs was the best. It was so pure you were tempted to drink it.

Claire and I amused ourselves in the evenings with board games. She had a closet full: Mousetrap, Operation, Mystery Date, you name it. Claire would quote the commercials while we played: "Roll the dice, move your mice." "Take out wrenched ankle." "Will he be a dream or a dud?" Claire cut out pictures from the front of Simplicity patterns so that I could play Mystery Date. The girl with blonde corkscrew pigtails, an embroidered peasant shirt, psychedelic culottes, and white knee socks was deemed the least desirable date. Claire had kept all her daughter's toys, among them a Frosty the Snowman Snow-Cone Maker with bottles of flavored syrup, an Easy Bake Oven, and an Etch-A-Sketch, on which we drew pictures of stiff, boxy cows and grinning bears sitting on boulders, warming their feet by small fires.

Claire and I enjoyed playing Yahtzee. She had a special fondness for it because she always won. In her hands those dice were quintuplets; in mine they were distant acquaintances, fellow integers adding up to zilch. Claire said it was because she believed in the power of numbers and patterns and claimed her luck was "all in the wrists." She had wrists that were unusually thin, as though they were an evolutionary legacy left by birds. I imagined her skeleton filled with air, weighted down by flesh, waiting to skin itself and ascend.

Once when I went looking for Claire to play a game of Parcheesi with me, I walked into her bedroom and found her clutching her knees and gulping air. There were pictures spread on the bed around her, spilling out of a Florsheim shoebox. Black-and-white snapshots of a man with a long face and thin waist, and a little girl patting a brown dog, eating cake, wearing shiny Mary Janes, sitting in a tiny pool. And one with Claire between the two, a light glowing behind them as though they were on fire, smiling, happily aflame. Somewhere in the neighborhood, a little girl began to sing scales. "Hear that?" Claire asked, looking at her knees. I patted her bare feet, hoping the child's singing would make her happy. "That's the sound a swan makes at the end of its life. They sing themselves to death." She gathered the photographs into her lap. "Only other swans can hear it, swans on the way out."

*   *   *

The only time I recall Claire ever getting angry with me—and it wasn't anger exactly—was the time in seventh grade when I brought Damita Davis home and we played Yahtzee and ate Vanilla Wafers. Claire looked on from the doorway as I rolled my way to a big victory. My wrists seemed to glow gold; I rubbed them between turns. It was the first time I'd ever won at Yahtzee. After the game, Claire shuffled out of the kitchen in her fuzzy lavender slippers and holed up in the bathroom. She stayed in there for two hours after Damita had gone home. When I finally dared to check on her, all I could see were her wrinkled, white fingers hanging over the edge of the bathtub and a meringue of pinned-up hair floating above the bubbles that rose up out of the tub like a dream. There were candles burnt down to pools of wax on saucers, and it smelled like the time we ironed Crayola shavings between pieces of waxed paper. The empty, wet and puckered box of Mr. Bubble beside the toilet alarmed me, I don't know why. Maybe it was just the sheer emptiness, ten baths' worth of bubbles extravagantly frothed for a single bathing. I flushed the toilet to cut the silence. Claire parted the foam with her hands, peering mystically through like a movie star in a soft-focus reverie.

"What?" she asked.

"I thought you were . . ."

"What?"

"Forget it. You're going to be a prune soon," I said.

"Do you love her?" she asked.

"Who?"

"You love her?"

"Damita? No! I think she let me win. I could never respect a woman like that." Claire gathered the bubbles around her again and sank out of view.

*   *   *

Nothing was ever really the same after the séance. At the time, it just seemed like a bitter bite, something she'd swallow and forget. Now I see it must have been a mouthful of disease.

The day of the séance, Claire was nervous and excited—the way I used to get before the Oak Grove Elementary school carnivals or the field trips to the Agricultural Hall of Fame. She picked red clover and daisies and marigolds and strewed them throughout the house like a fertility goddess. She even floated some bachelor's buttons in the cat's water. She took everything elevated and breakable off shelves and tables—plates, lamps, clocks, candlesticks—and laid them on the floor, as if she were anticipating a quake. She explained that the collision of the spirit realm with the physical world was known to send actual vibrations all through the house and sometimes beyond. Claire was cautious and reverent when it came to consorting with spirits.

We decided we would try to contact my mother, since she was the only dead person we had in common. Claire made me take a bath, wash my hair, and dress up in my stiff suit even though it was hot and the suit made me itch. She had a high regard for those who now knew "the geography of death." Mrs. Moody, a spiritually compatible customer of Claire's, joined us in hope of hooking up with her late brother, Harold. We sat around the kitchen table and grinned politely at one another for a while, pointing at the bird feeder outside the kitchen window whenever anything more colorful than a starling alighted.

Finally Claire told me to fetch my clackers—two translucent lavender balls with flecks of foil inside. Each ball dangled from a string. You held the clackers by a plastic ring and snapped them up and down, clacking them together, faster and faster until they looked like fluttering wings. I hadn't played with them since a kid at school told me a boy in Saint Louis clacked his a little too hard, and they splintered and flew into his eyes. My mother had given them to me on my sixth birthday. I'm sure she'd had no inkling they'd prove to be dangerous. She also gave me a small, plastic Scrooge McDuck that collapsed in a heap when you pressed on his foundation, snapping back into shape when you released it. Claire thought the clackers would be a better spiritual conduit than the duck.

We all held hands. Claire dangled the clackers between our clasped hands, and Mrs. Moody held a flat, soiled rabbit fashioned out of braided pipe cleaners between ours. She had fat little link-sausage fingers that bulged out of an already sweating palm. She smiled apologetically as we locked fingers, but I didn't mind the sweat because she smelled like cookies. We all closed our eyes, and Mrs. Moody started humming "Amazing Grace." She sang the words *but now am found* and *but now I see* aloud and then stopped.

After a few moments of silence, Claire's grip tightened, and I felt her arm stiffen. When my hand began to go numb, I breached séance etiquette and looked over at Claire. I saw a thread of blood trailing from her lip where she was biting it. I saw that Mrs. Moody was looking too. She was staring at her clenched hand, which was white and bloodless and would probably turn the bluish color of her hair before long—hair Claire herself had recently colored and styled. Neither of us said a word. We were afraid to disturb Claire in this state, as though she were sleepwalking among the dead and in peril of being trapped in a limbo world if roused.

As Claire walked among spirits, I thought about my mother's hands; they were soft as flannel. Sometimes at night as I fell asleep, she would rub my feet and talk about movie stars. She told

64

me she had always been a little bit in love with Cary Grant and knew if he met her, he would want to buy her a pair of black satin pumps. She felt certain Dana Andrews paid his bills long before they were due and invested his money wisely. Gene Tierney, she said, would certainly go out of her way to care for limping dogs and fallen birds, despite what some of the vixenish roles she'd played might make you think of her. After these stories, I often dreamt of large and kind and beautiful people who brought food wrapped in tinfoil to our house or gladly drove us, in cars with seats as soft as feathers, anywhere we wanted to go. I wondered if my mother would remember any of this or if she had left her earthly recollections behind.

Claire let out an explosive gasp, like someone long submerged bursting to the surface of a lake. Mrs. Moody screamed, and I kicked over the bowl of plastic fruit at my feet. Claire sat stone still until Mrs. Moody asked in a trembling voice, "Did you see Mrs. Yulich?"

Claire turned her gaze to Mrs. Moody, but her expression remained fixed. "She's dead," Claire said. She turned to me and said, "You're to sleep in your own room tonight."

I can't be sure if Claire made contact because it was never mentioned again, but I think she experienced something on the other side that pained her terribly. Maybe she saw my mother weeping. My mother cried so quietly, you could tell she was crying only by the rounded shape of her shoulders. It always made me wish I could step out of my skin and wrap her in it. Maybe Claire saw my mother crying, quiet as a sick child.

*   *   *

The good days grew less and less frequent after that. Claire gradually phased out her beauty business and withdrew from me too. She forbade me to go in her bedroom unless she wasn't in it, which was increasingly rare. Tiny wrinkles began collecting around her eyes and mouth, as if she hadn't allowed them until now. She began drinking her coffee with heaping spoonfuls of sugar, and she chewed her fingers until they bled. But sometimes she'd sit in the garden and pull weeds and seem strong and steady in her dirty dress and rubber shoes.

*　*　*

One day, after an extended period of brooding silence, Claire snapped out of it just like that, like Scrooge McDuck, as though strings in her limbs had been pulled suddenly taut. It was a Saturday, and I was watching *Lancelot Link* on television. Claire and I used to sit together on Saturdays and I'd watch her straining face as she tried not to laugh. She claimed the star of the show, a trained chimp, was my first cousin and always remarked on the family resemblance. On this day, she swept into my room like a warm wind and cupped my face in her hands. She began kissing my fingers and wrists and pecked her way up to my closed eyes. It was a startling change, and I was afraid to move. She laughed out loud and drew me to her, patting my back gently.

"Things are going to be different," she said, looking into my eyes, trying on different grins as she stared into them, as if she had just gotten a new mouth and was testing its range. "Let's go to that new Exotic Animal Drive-Thru Paradise. What do you say? I hear they have bears!"

So we packed a picnic lunch and headed for the park, ignoring the silence, the days and months of anxious quiet that had preceded this transformation. On the way there, we sang with the radio, honked at the grazing cows, and kept track of out-of-state license plates, like we used to. Claire even laughed for the first time in a long time when I imitated Buck, the German shepherd that was poisoned, by hanging out the window, licking the air, snapping at bugs, and threatening to jump.

When we got to the park, a man in a safari hat and leopard-spotted scarf gave us a map and told us to keep our windows rolled up at all times because of the bears. He said not to try to feed them no matter how friendly or harmless they might appear.

We traveled down a road identified as Mallard Avenue on the map. We didn't see anything but trees for quite a stretch. Finally, we saw a large herd of sheep grazing near a pond.

"Pretty exotic," Claire said. One side of her mouth was pursed.

They looked like clouds on legs from a distance. As we got closer, we could see their chewing faces, and I said, "Maybe they'd let you fix their hair." Claire had always shamelessly solicited customers wherever we went, though she claimed to target only the choicest coifs.

"Those mops?" she said. "That would require sheer talent, hardy har," We both laughed, a foreign sound. It felt good to laugh together again, a feeling of convalescence or release like we'd just gotten over a malingering cold or out of an interminable winter.

We turned onto Bison Boulevard. The map made it appear as if this were the wildlife hub. We didn't see anything but some ducks and a couple of deer for the first few hundred feet, then we saw brown, white, and black bodies bumping along the road ahead. As they came into view, we could see they were llamas. We pulled off to the side and stopped in the grass. There was a huddle of llamas a few feet in front of us, and they kept turning around and looking at us as though they were gossiping. The group dispersed, strategically it seemed, and one of the rust-colored llamas walked toward our car. It walked over to Claire's side and looked straight in at her. Claire knocked against the window, but it just stood there staring at her, then it pressed its mouth and nose against the window and slobbered on it.

"Think he wants a tip," Claire said, and she rolled down the window and offered him a shelled peanut. He took it gently from her hands with his thick, sticky lips and tongue.

In spite of the injunction to "keep the windows rolled up," we decided to have our picnic at this site, beneath the cloak of a large weeping-willow tree. Claire found the llamas soothing. As we spread out beneath the tree, we could see two peacocks sauntering toward us. We ate grapes, cheese and crackers, celery stuffed with peanut butter, marshmallows, and we each had a can of lukewarm grape Nehi. As the peacocks came closer, Claire threw out a handful of pastel-colored miniature marshmallows. The birds came near us, but walked on the marshmallows without interest, as though they were only cushioned stones, unworthy of scrutiny. They stopped once they got safely past us, fanned out in the sun, arched their necks, and I imagined they were absorbing energy and color through the eyes in their tails. I imagined they'd lift up in the air and spin colorfully like fireworks.

As we stretched out on our backs, three llamas inched cautiously closer and cleaned up the marshmallows. Then they stood there with stiffened ears, looking at us, baring their big teeth, perhaps waiting for second helpings. One of them hissed at us, and Claire hissed back, causing them all to back up. Claire reached into the picnic basket and pulled out a box of powdered sugar. She pushed my T-shirt up around my shoulders and sprinkled the sugar on my stomach carefully, as if I were a cookie. She pulled out some strawberries and rolled them in the sugar. The llamas looked on like big, curious dogs, dipping their noses and sniffing the air as we ate. When we had eaten all the strawberries, Claire licked the remaining sugar off my stomach, and my muscles tensed. She laid her head on the moist circle.

"I can hear your intestines laboring," she said. She traced a winding path along my stomach with her finger. "The food sprouts, grows, takes shape, and we eat it. It changes and is passed along to feed the earth. It assumes a new form, a radish, a pear, and we eat it again. We could be partaking of the organic leftovers of . . . Akhenaton . . . Fatty Arbuckle . . ."

"Who?"

"We could be breaking bread with Christ in a manner of speaking." Claire sat up and gently kissed my eyebrows, my nose. "Do you suppose resurrection disqualifies him?" she asked. "How human was he really, if there was no putrefaction?" She leaned on her elbow and twisted my hair around her finger.

"Life is an endless meal, a banquet, and this moment, this succulent moment, is merely a bite." My stomach lurched. This was an observation Claire had been fond of making, but in her privation the metaphor had not been apt for a long time. I wondered if it could last, if she'd savor that arm-in-arm companionship again, if it would be like before when the warmth we shared—each of us clumsily reckoning with loss—kept the boxed-up memories from haunting her, from making her sit so still and dead, staring at her knees, our intimacy interrupted by phantoms whose sternness she buckled beneath. I missed the feeling of her hand on my stomach.

And then I imagined choking on a bad day, the unpleasant hours sliding down my windpipe, blocking my breath as I struggled to dislodge them. As I lay there thinking, a black-and-white zebra-striped jeep pulled up and parked behind our car. A man dressed from head to toe in khaki stepped out and shined a flashlight at us, as though the beam would hold us in place. It shone through the drooping branches, competing with the threads of sunlight that embroidered our faces. We sat up. Claire positioned her head in the light's path and stared into it.

"You folks are clearly in violation here," the man said, lowering the flashlight. "It states right there on your ticket that you are not under any circumstances to get out of your car. In so doing, you have jeopardized your own lives as well as the welfare of the park and do hereby relinquish your rights as guests. I must escort you out of the park immediately. Your tickets are nonrefundable." The words came out of his mouth rapid and shaky. I could tell it was a speech that he had long waited for the opportunity to make and now that it was over, a look of letdown crimped his face.

"I am not frightened of peacocks or llamas," Claire said in a formal drawl. "Nor they of me."

"You are very near the wild boars' favorite watering hole. They're a rough lot, them boars. They'd just as soon skewer you as look at you," he said.

"*I've* only seen llamas and peacocks and assorted barnyard stock," Claire said, as she stood and smoothed her dress.

"I bet you don't even have any old bears," I said.

"We have bears. Just because you didn't see them doesn't mean we don't have bears. They don't appear on demand. We *have* bears."

I'd hit a nerve.

"Please gather your things, get in your car, and follow me out of the park."

Just before we came to the exit gate displaying a sign that read THANK YOU FOR VISITING THE EXOTIC ANIMAL PARADISE. HOPE YOU HAD AN UN**BEAR**ABLY GOOD TIME, the man in the truck pointed his arm out the window at a dense stand of trees in the distance. "Bears!" he yelled, as we drove out.

*　*　*

That afternoon was the last savory bite Claire and I shared. It seemed the moment we arrived home, the day became instantly something to be filed away in a mental scrapbook. Claire tried hard to hold on to her good humor, but she quickly lost all resolve. The bitter bites came back, consumed her. Or her soul had decided to fast. Sometimes I could see her face straining so to form a smile, thoughtful with effort, as though it were heaving an anvil. I held Claire's slack and thinning body to mine, felt the sharpness of her shoulders, tried to be bone and muscle to her. I imagined pushing my hand inside Claire, straight through her navel and into the nucleus of her history, casting out sad pictures and making more room for her god—the god of a glorious growth you could hear if attuned—to take root. I imagined something cool and small at the center, something untouched by pain or memory or shame, and I clasped it in my hands, a shriveled seed, tried to shore up the last fragments of an ailing spirit.

* * *

Some months after the trip to the animal park, she agreed to go to a movie.

Fantasia was playing at the Bijou. Claire moved slowly about the rooms of the house as the steps of grooming came back to her one by one. She dabbed circles of rouge on her dry cheeks and pinned knotted curls back with a pearl-studded comb. She pressed a flowered dress and found a pocketbook the same watery blue as the petals. Claire had grown so thin, the dress hung on her. There was only a faint suggestion of body beneath the fabric. You could see through her skin that even her spirit was withered. Claire's eyes were wide open, wet and restless with longing. I felt sure the movie would bring her back to me, hungry, joyful.

As the coming attractions played, two young girls sat down in front of us. Claire, who had been speaking of the plush comfort of the theater seats, became quiet again. She smiled periodically and nodded at me, twisted her hair, fingered the pearls on the comb. When the movie began, I looked over to see if it registered any expression on Claire's face. She was staring at the back of one of the girls' heads. I reached over and took Claire's hand in both of mine. I smoothed and patted her arm as though trying to tame it. She pulled away and reached into her purse, took out a brush. She leaned forward and freed the girl's hair from the back of the chair. The girl turned slowly around, looked at Claire, then locked her gaze on me. Claire brushed the long blonde strands in her hand. I half-smiled at the girl, as if I had just asked her for a favor. She turned back around and sat perfectly still as Claire stroked her hair. The other girl turned and stared at Claire, who grinned down at the rope of hair in her hands.

The subtle music behind the movie changed abruptly, bellowing deeply and thumping beneath our feet. I heard someone behind me ask, "Where are the words? When are they going to say something?" Claire dropped the hair and stood up. She stared absently at the screen. Popcorn hit her back. She apologized to the people sitting next to us and moved to the aisle, walked toward the screen. People in the audience turned to look at her and began whispering. She walked up the steps at the side of the stage. The audience became audibly hushed. She walked to the center of the screen and raised her hand to it. Mickey Mouse capered about, ankle deep in water, a pail in his hands. He scrambled frantically through Claire's shadow, sweeping the water away. Claire gracefully eased herself to the floor like a falling leaf. A battalion of angry brooms marched above her. Some of the kids in the audience clapped, others giggled, and some threw empty candy boxes at the stage. I caught the worried eye of the blonde girl who was seated in front of us as I walked down the aisle. When I reached Claire, I knelt beside her and put my hand on her forehead. The projectionist stopped the film, houselights came on, and teenaged ushers rushed toward us and stopped short, uncertain. Claire looked at me, at my mouth. She licked her lips. "I can't taste a thing," she said.

*   *   *

After that Claire and I lived together in silence, Claire's hunched figure deforming into a shape of increasing resignation and sorrow

I couldn't—or didn't want to—make out. I fed her and bathed her, read her stories from *Life* magazine about the world's transformations and setbacks, and sometimes she'd smile, shake her head. One day, at the instigation of a concerned neighbor, two men and a woman dressed in crisp, white clothing came and took Claire away. They held her by the arms and escorted her into a van. She offered no resistance.

*　*　*

I visited her once—last year, June 29, my seventeenth birthday. It wasn't Claire really, just a facsimile, a loose satchel of cells unable to cage the roaming soul, fled, in search of soiled seraphim. I wouldn't know where to begin looking for the Claire I'd known. In the garden, maybe, clinging to the slick pink and green underside of a rhubarb leaf. In the scraps of earth, the dirt beneath my fingernails. Or maybe drinking a soda with friends in heaven, waiting to be born again. Hibernating like bears in a drive-through paradise, napping in inaccessible places.

A nurse told me she'd become fully unresponsive and they were forced to feed her through a tube. She'd shed all superfluous gestures, one by one. Claire and I sat together quietly, her eyes looking past me, weary with the onus of sight, her gaze resting on my shoulder. I put my finger between her dry lips and pressed against her teeth. She parted her teeth slightly and I waited, hoped for the gentle pressure of her bite. I closed my eyes and listened for distant singing, listened for signs of invisible growth happening somewhere in the world.

Star-dogged Moon

This is form gulping after formlessness,
Skin flashing to wished-for disappearances
And the serpent body flashing without skin.

WALLACE STEVENS

I wasn't always as I am now, ugly, distorted, features culminating in a disordered aspect. Wasn't always deserving of the averted gazes that carom off my own straight-ahead stare. Sometimes I catch only the end of the movement, the head arcing away, but it is as familiar to me as my hands—the part of the body a person sees most, clasped or dangling so often in the vicinity of one's distracted stare, a strikingly fine feature amid the mess of me— and I am past trying to see the repulsion as a random gesture ungrounded in me, my twisted asymmetry. Discerning eyes prefer to crawl along swollen gutters, settle on the fur-tufted asses of dogs waddling in front of them, study the dying ivy on buildings. There was a period of several months when I was three years old in which I possessed an openhanded, searching charm that drew people to me. My mother says I had the airy beauty of something fleeting, features smeared hastily across a face soon to expire, and I waved my arms about in what seemed to her the hurried delight of a short lifespan. I still seem to her like someone who won't be staying, though I persist, impudently, against her most studied calculations.

It is my father who escaped prematurely, as I always knew that he would. He'd been walking the knife blade between living and dying most of his life and was always tilted slightly toward extinction. The temptation not to exist was strong in my father, and I knew his body would use any excuse to take him from me, render him a grainy Polaroid in a photo album—a man walking away, waving goodbye, face blurred in turning, hand on his fedora—reduce him to a commemorative mum pressed between the leaves of a dictionary, scenting the words between *Easter egg* and *ecce homo* with that funereal perfume. He often told me I was a splendid child, and I knew he meant to reassure me about the effects of his impending absence. I knew I was meant to continue to see myself through his snuffed-out eyes, see the dazzling *Astrum* he insisted I was, my soubriquet. This was before my own body gave protest.

As a small child, I would often wake in the night in winter and steal into my parents' bedroom, quietly lay my head on my father's flanneled chest, feel the swell and breath that would reassure me of another day's stay against the extinction of my father. I carried the breeze of his sleeping breaths against my forehead with me back to bed. Sometimes I'd hear my mother rouse, and I imagined her sitting up briskly and fixing me with an accusing stare, catching the flounce of my exiting nightgown, halting me, the hot coals of her eyes glowing gold in the dark and boring from behind into the feckless heart of her monster daughter, impatient with my continuing shape. Sometimes I would stay, breathe stealthy half-breaths, lie beside my father on the floor and listen for fatal shifts.

My mother was young when I unexpectedly appeared in her womb, an irritating kernel of sand, one no amount of pearly cocooning could rescue, make soothing, one whose subtle chafe she continues to try to expel, so young, my mother, that she could never fully persuade herself of the idea of me, having only recently come to hard terms with the theory of herself. I am now the full-grown phantom reminder of the discomfort of those months, and she occasionally groans or pants when I am near, holds a hand to her abdomen. My mother is like those resurrectionists of the nineteenth century, perfunctorily grisly anatomists exhuming fresh bodies in pursuit of knowledge, understanding, a ravenous reckoning of flesh and science. My mother digs me up and digs me up, turns me over in her hands, brushes the soil from my withered face, and tries to grasp the consequences of feelings that well up more quickly than reason.

Don't misunderstand. My mother is a remarkable woman with a remarkable heart that beats so loudly and steadily it is difficult to think in her presence. She campaigns for the freedom of oppressed peoples; she dresses wounds on fields of battle; she dispenses the alms of her soul indiscriminately to the spiritually parched. Every minute a new and extraordinary idea surfaces in her mind, like the stoppered bottle of a long-traveled revelation bobbing to the surface. It is only that I am never one of them.

At supper, I often stared at my father's wingtip shoes beneath the table and imagined him taking flight, lifting into the air, upside down, coins and golf tees and shoehorn jingling free and falling to the kitchen floor. I saw his handkerchief flutter down and cover my small head like a wimple, the monogrammed PK resting on my forehead, a symbol of the caste to which I was pledged, imagined grabbing his hand and disappearing into the ether with him, sealed into a safe eternity, a place where anonymity is common and where we would be easily happy and sated, unimposing, sleeping near the heat of small fires.

I met a man, Jack, who said he might be able to love me if he shifted his standards a little. He fashioned small figures from clay and sold them on the streets. I modeled for him in his basement apartment in an unflattering light. He had Manichaean hands that shaped vague objects, objects people could not help stopping to revile, molten shapes that were only the outward contours of a festering interior and that attested to the wisdom of leaving this plane as expeditiously as possible, suffering through it only until God bent closer and inhaled us away to the narcotic beauty of the Other Side. Sometimes he hissed at children as they passed, could not tolerate what he saw as the specious argument of their elongating limbs and ease, and they threw stones at him and ran. I was both repelled by and attracted to him, these displays. Children have always confused me. I felt he was helping to clarify my future.

My father died on the morning of my seventh birthday, January 7. It was his heart. It's always the heart, isn't it, even when it's not? Ultimately. He died in the hospital on a gurney with squeaking wheels, having been spirited into an emergency room where a flurry of people in green, trained and dutifully sterilized for such foregone conclusions, tried to inflate the congested arteries of his heart. My mother and I watched on a waiting-room monitor hung from the ceiling as a tiny balloon lodged itself in a major estuary near the failing muscle. My mother signed the appropriate papers, consigning the body to the local funeral home, and we returned home before lunch. As I sat at the kitchen table, I wondered what I should do with my winter nights without my father to watch over. My mother's breathing was never in question. I knew she could inhale smoke and water and survive and would likely continue to breathe long after death, confounding science and God and bereavement, so would never require the talisman—now proven to be ineffectual—of my vigils to sustain her through to eternity. She had resources the rest of us dared not even contemplate lest we let go the ghost on the spot out of sheer startled appreciation of the disparity. There was no limit to that skin-deep vitality, which seemed to be stored in her very glands, emitted strategically, a musk that drew the wounded to her. Next to the dim light we shed, the corona encircling her burned all the more brightly.

She set before me a small layer cake with pink icing, red gumdrops, and six lit candles. (*Six* candles—I was being stalled.) She smiled and tucked my hair behind my ears, hummed the birthday song, pushed the celebration of my birth through, yoking it with loss, with latent finalities, and my capacity for joy has since, as you might imagine, been vexed. I ate the cake silently, the muscles in my small body suddenly taut and straining against the skin that seemed to serve only to keep them from leaping from bone into space, scattering cells in all directions, but my bladder relaxed and I soiled my new red stirrup pants. My mother peeled them from me and threw them into the trash with the remains of the cake, and I spent the rest of the afternoon in my room, watching neighborhood dogs pad across our front yard and leave crisscrossing footprints in the melting crust of snow, explorers circling their own tracks, possessed of an arctic fever.

*   *   *

Somehow there were enough people in the grip of a disconsolate vision that Jack was able to sustain himself on the proceeds from the sale of his figures. His overhead was exceedingly low, living as he did in a dank efficiency in a low-rent neighborhood threatening in its conspicuous indigence—thin people with shoulders hunched against the weather in all seasons, circling the blocks, ragtag except for new sneakers, pitching cigarette butts at the rusting carcasses of cars, eyes open only wide enough to discern if there was a reason to look—threatening to anyone who had anything to lose. Jack did not believe in debt or possessions, and his apartment was furnished with only a kitchen chair and parson's table, which had to be stacked and wedged when the Murphy bed descended from the wall. The snug fit of his apartment demanded at every moment a singularity of purpose. He had one dish, one glass, fork, knife, and spoon, a hot plate, and we never shared a meal together. It is not unthinkable that he chose me for my spare, if disfigured, frame, the fact that I could easily squeeze myself between his scant belongings, would not claim much room in a life quitted of accumulation, strategically lightened and ready for flight, and would never ask for sustenance.

Jack could scarcely conceal his pride over never having owned a book. He felt words were vulgar, dealt an irreparable violence to the essence they symboled, and wanted as little truck with them as possible. I often watched him as he stared, dazed and unwitting neo-Platonist, into space, wordlessly tracking, I imagined, the shimmer of origin beneath that swollen emptiness, that hoodwinking veneer, his mind filled with a joyful buzzing. He spoke, of course, and not with particular economy but in such a tone as to make you think that a gathering incipience had been given expression—the start of something that would rend you if allowed to move to conclusion—leaving you with the sole and aching ambition of somehow finding yourself intact on the other side of the befuddled suffering that cadenced his every word, his voice a test of preternatural mettle. Sometimes my courage flagged and I fixed my hearing on the clatter in the alley.

In the absence of my father, my mother and I lived together in our split-level home happily chilled by the central air-conditioning installed by my father at the end of the previous summer—a stretch of weeks that broke both meteorological and cooling systems sales records and that instantly scorched the exposed skins of all who ventured outside shade or shelter—high-powered air conditioning guaranteed to tame the heat of even the wildest August. Sometimes I stood beside the whirring generator in the backyard and leaned my face into the hot exhalations of its rushing breath.

On sweltering afternoons, I lay on my bed and felt the time bomb of my genes tick-ticking inside me. What internal skirmish would be waged in this meet of congenital surrender and gallingly halcyon fortitude? My knees and hips and elbows throbbed with such regularity I imagined there were tiny, diseased hearts stowed inside the joints, and I tensed my muscles against the ache. The pain coiled inside my bones; I gnawed at my lip. Somehow my mother always sensed this private growth, sensed my skeleton yearning to exceed the straitjacket of skin, and she brought a bowl of ice into my room and rubbed the dripping cubes along my shins, held them fast against my kneecaps. The air in my room was already chilled to a wintry defiance of the over-baked atmosphere outside, and my body responded to this ice bath with instant gooseflesh. She would freeze me, halt my body in its tracks, keep me from displacing more air than I already did. I tried to sink back into my impertinent bones as I had watched my father do. This chronic growth seemed more than either my mother or I could suffer.

It often happened that as I sat at the small drafting table in my room, tracing the outlines of my hands and feet onto colorful leaves of construction paper or writing tall words with a fat pencil onto the pages of wide-ruled tablets—TREE, FEET, CLEAN—something in the act would strike me as comic—the blue splay of fingers, the assonant camaraderie of the words—and I would laugh out loud, sometimes with such conviction that my mother would suddenly appear in front of me, alarmed, armed with comfort, having mistaken the laughter for sobbing. She'd march into my room, her eyes flickering with sharp poniards of good cheer with which she meant to stab me. That I was in no need of consolation would at times seem to her an affront, and she would push my knees together, hold my hands tightly, and look solemnly into my eyes, waiting for the need to arise. Superfluous gestures bent her spirit, prizing as she did a certain devout thrift of thought and action with regard to mothering, and therefore any instance of being stirred, however slightly, necessarily required that the movement end in the establishment of a definite and fitting provocation, which, to her dismay, she was never able on these occasions to locate in my face, incapable, unlike the rest of me, of dissembling, and so would eventually have to seek elsewhere an outlet for a pity unnecessarily piqued, in the kitchen or basement, among moldering things.

One winter night, my mother took me outside and showed me the moon. She presented it with snapped-open hands—ta-daa!—an unveiling, and I saw the mantle slip from it and drift sidelong through the frosty air. "The moon is your ally," she said. "Sometimes it will tug at you, yank you into pain. Here," she said and pressed my abdomen below the navel. "You'll want to mark this on a calendar and pay attention to the rhythm of the ache. Every nurse you ever meet will carry a clipboard and pen for the express purpose of recording this date. There may be times when you wish to be free of this ailment, but you'll be grateful, later, for its return."

"And the stars?" I asked. On this night, the sky glittered.

"If you're careful, you'll never need worry about them," she said. "You see there are too many to be fed. There's only so much any one moon can do."

The night before my father gave way to the pull of the lodestone I imagined death was for him, I stood at the door of his study and watched him as he sat in his oxblood bergère. He sat hunched in a contemplative C, sunk into the leather with his legs crossed and a highball clasped limply in one hand. He wore a black turtleneck and trousers, and in the dusky light, through squinting eyes, it appeared as though he was only head and hands floating above the chair. A package of balloons sat in his lap. He set his drink down and took a blue balloon from the package. He blew rattling breaths into the balloon, knotted it off, and batted it across the room. I heard my mother's sure steps behind me and I moved inside the room, sidestepped to a darkened corner. My mother stood in the doorway, her hands hanging at her sides. She never felt compelled to pose or engage any part of her body in activity for the sheer sake of cutting a figure. My father lifted his drink in the air and smiled.

The next day, after we returned from the hospital, I went back into the study, found the balloon, and pulled at its throat until the Adam's apple of the knot came free. I inhaled my father's breath, took the contagion into my lungs, and there he was seeded.

When I'm feeling miscellaneous, I think of you, Jack, and your sister, think of the afflicted glamour of the suicide, whose legend is staked on sudden absence, that decisive surrender to permanent anonymity that leads to notice. That's where I met you, at your sister's funeral. She had sat in the cubicle next to mine at the insurance agency we both worked for, me temporarily. Her too as it turned out. She had health benefits, vision and dental inclusive, an ergonomic chair, shorter stacks of paper in her trays, and I envied her, though such rewards required a reconciliation to each day twinning itself endlessly that I'd not yet arrived at. The building we worked in was fashioned entirely of a monotony of square plates of reflective glass, a monument to blinding light and the transparent future that lies ahead of something as small and unassuming as sand. A fortune had been spent on jalousies, but at our station, the blinds remained hitched, and we both stared out at the people below us scurrying across the concrete plaza, people feeding pigeons as they talked on floating phones. I did not know your sister well but was not surprised to learn that over a three-day weekend she lay on a pillow on her kitchen floor and pulled gas into her lungs until she no longer needed to make decisions. On Thursday, personal objects—Ansel Adams calendar, ficus, fountain pen, bottle of Waterman blue ink—were cleared from your sister's desk by a woman I'd never seen before, an emissary from Human Resources, apparently trained in such labor, who quietly dropped the blinds, looked at me consolingly, and squeezed my shoulder when she left. A certain tightness around her eyes as she paused behind my chair and looked down at me seemed to suggest she felt it was only a matter of time before I took similar initiative. I felt vaguely nettled by her touch and the absence of officiousness in the manner in which she carried your sister's possessions away. It was distressingly intimate, how she held the small box to her breast, an anonymous gray carton housing those diffident expressions of office self turned detritus in the wake of erasure, the termination of a person this woman had likely met only once, if at all. One of the advantages of working for a large insurance company in a showy glass building downtown in the refurbished center of commerce is that you know just what to expect from human interaction and therefore are rarely put upon to improvise.

At night before I leave you, your lips move as you breathe, clicking susurrus of agitated longing into my ear (so I persuade myself), the busy legs of captive crickets as they saw their music in the dark, and I imagine I have a face everyone could love. The chaste and unconscious travel of your hand across my stomach is the gesture of a species happily endangering itself.

*   *   *

The terror of childhood is, to the adult, an ordinary thing, a wilderness domesticated. But to the child, all experience can be deliciously monstrous. I walked outside feeling like a dream, having been awake only a short while. It was early May and the air was warm and honeyed with the smell of new flowers. I observed a fine powder floating in the air and sensed a distinct change had taken place overnight, the atmosphere slightly recalibrated to suit the wanderings of airier beings. The sky looked temporary in its exaggerated blueness. It made my eyes itch to look at it. It appeared to me as though it had been holding its breath and if it would only exhale, it was sure to lighten to a more bearable shade. There was no one else outside, no dogs, no cars passing. The houses seemed thin and uncertain, wavy with heat, and I walked across the street to knock on Karla Hauser's front door but became afraid I might knock it flat, might be crushed if it fell the wrong way. Suddenly I felt a coldness stirring inside me, starting beneath the skin of my arms and traveling through my stomach and legs toward the deepest, most fugitive part of me. I stood directly in full sunlight with my arms stretched out to catch the warmth and began to shake. I felt the heat around me but could not reach it, was capsuled inside it yet unable to escape the blizzard within me. I began to burn, a punished witch, swinging between climatic extremes, smelled the charred flesh of my feet. I ran to the chain-link fence that separated the neighbor's yard from ours. I fingered the vines of morning glories, tried to concentrate on the feeling in my fingertips as I traced the winding green growth through the metal links, but the tundra spread quickly through me and I bloodied my tongue when my icy teeth began to chatter. I gawked at the bright blue belly above me and waited for it to breathe out and warm me, warm me! But I felt my skin splitting, the overripe pod of me; my stomach wobbled, and I ran inside the house, covered myself with the scratchy black afghan on the couch, happy to tremble beneath its prickly warmth, though it was a reassurance that did little to shield me from the chill gale that whistled through my ribs. I held my feet and counted.

My mother explained fever to me and used calamine lotion to dim the red bumps on my sweating face and arms to a chalky pink and my father fed me soupy ice cream, but they focused on points behind me as they sat before me and held my hands and told me how damaged I'd be if I scratched. I turned around and thought I saw another little girl there, smiling agreeably, shiny shoes, a girl covered with fresh and temperate skin, warm in any weather.

On nights when the moon spills through my window and covers my bare legs, spreads up my abdomen like infection, I watch the cells of my body cleave neatly at the perforations and swarm above me like silver bees. I watch the powdery motes of self floating in the light, and I know that when these glinting particles have had their fill of autonomy and reconvene into a putty resembling me, the outline will be a hair's breadth altered, an atom or two gone AWOL, and I'll never be the same. There's always of course the danger that full-scale mutiny will occur and I'll salt the air indefinitely. My mother will come into my room in the morning, dust me from the dresser, and shake me out the window as I settle on her impermeable skin, squatter.

It is my twenty-eighth birthday and I meet my mother at a new restaurant. She wears a cream-colored cardigan sweater draped over her shoulders and a light-green silk blouse. She has just come from the children's hospital where she volunteers, rocking to sleep or smoothing the yellow cheeks of jittery infants who've inherited disease or addiction from mothers, newborns not statistically well favored, struggling beneath inauspicious origins and a blank futurity. People at the hospital think highly of my mother. She's in real estate now and has aided all manner of hospital personnel in their gentrified or modest-income dreams of opulent or affordable housing. She gathers them all into her heart and finds a place where each will feel happy and settled. She reports to me their gratitude, shows me the cards and small gifts, the baskets of baked goods.

We are seated near a window, my preference, and I wait for my mother to shiver and request a less drafty arrangement. The air that surrounds us is warm and unmoving, but my mother chills instantly within an arm's length of panes of clear glass. I imagine they must somehow call her attention to her own body in a way she cannot abide. And she does not like to be framed, does not like her static elegance to be bordered and gilded, viewed from outside.

Outside the sky is stained an indelible black and the moon rises unblinking. I am of a mind to put out the sky's fat eye, blind its Cyclops glower, throw a pencil at it and run, so that it might stop following me, stop making me small. Dogging the moon is a star (though really it is not so easy to say who is on the heel of whom), a chip of pulsating light, its progeny. I wish I were a wary mariner so I could fear such harbingers of rough-waved peril, but for me, forever moored to dry land, it carries no notable portent (though I'm still capable, of course, of pricking myself with metaphorical conclusions). I was raised in such a way as to respond reasonably to the world, not to be jacklighted by fishy mythologies, like death and moons and motherhood or millenarian hullabaloos, and so no longer register every inscrutable tremor, am insensitive to the duping woof and warp of things around me, no longer feel the febrile flush of my own cheeks, and this contributes to a strategic inconcinnity that keeps me from attracting passing spectacles or dubiously vaulted sentiments.

(Actually, this is not at all true. Sometimes I am so plagued by fancy that I have time for little else.)

You cannot know how desperately I love my mother.

"You're looking peaked," says my mother. She does not appear disapproving. She looks at me quizzically, as though I were a slice of urban development she were trying to appraise. From the slant of her lips, I surmise I would generate a paltry commission. I do this, I commodify myself through my mother's eyes, see myself as a bad risk in a frozen market. She cannot be blamed for this habit. I'm not sure she can be blamed for anything. She seems to be staring at my cheek, near my ear, at the faint scar left behind by the chicken pox. She is perhaps wondering why I have tucked my hair behind my ears. That is, after all, at least one blemish that could so easily be concealed.

My mother slides a card across the table. There is nothing written on the envelope and the flap is tucked inside, unsealed. On the card is a pair of morbidly obese adult identical twins in Shirley Temple curls and patent-leather shoes, wearing sailor suits and holding layer cakes. The photograph is black and white except for the blue, white, and red of the sailor suits, the airbrushed apples of their cheeks, and the yellow candles on the cakes. The printed message inside says *Happy Birthday, Big Girl!* I feel my stomach toss, as though it had lost its footing. My mother smiles at me conspiratorially, as she always does on my birthday, and I feel vague.

*   *   *

The Day of Ascension will one day come, a momentous day for Jack, and I watch him now as he sleeps, eyes already jerking beneath thin lids, hands trembling. I wish to help him prepare to rise, to beat the corporeal rap, and I decide to stare him into heaven, hoist him up with the crane of my riveted gaze, the way magicians coax grinning assistants up toward hot stage-lights, making their stiff bodies hum beneath pink satin skirts hanging down as they float. The beams of my eyes are the thick tines of a forklift that slip beneath Jack's body and make him stiffen, the cold, hard metal of my stare. It's easy: he's light as meringue, my taut eyes barely register the heft, so I lift him into the air, sheet and blanket falling free, the body birthed from mundane slumber

87

into a somnambulistic hover diminishing the distance between dream and eternity, and press him against the ceiling, urging him toward the limits of matter, until his face instinctively turns to the side and his cheek meets the haphazardly spackled fractures that creep across his ceiling like a slow quake. He begins to stir and I let him descend, rocking gently, a tossed feather. I stare at his face. His cheek is pocked red like mine as a child during illness: beautifully ruined.

I disappear into views of myself I've somewhere inherited. I master the fraud by swelling the deformity so that it is as distinct as DNA, not merely a pedestrian hand-me-down. I believe we are neither who we're told we are nor who we deceive ourselves into believing we are, and the single consolation to be had is in grasping this, that we cannot be known. Despite this, there is of course the constant dread of being finally apprehended, the cipher of being cracked like dropped crockery to reveal the absence the fictions are meant to swaddle (the emperor himself, and not his airy vestments, being the real swindle), but really I think there is little to worry about.

On this night, I meet the ample twins of my mother's card in my dreams. I know that dreams mean both nothing and everything and this tallies with my general waking experience, so I neither dismiss them nor find them telling. Perhaps the trick is simply being able to accurately identify which antipodes you shuttle between. The twins ride unicycles on high-wires so burdened they sag nearly to the ground, but this does not prevent the crowd, which I hear but cannot see, from gasping when the balancing baton of one of the twins tips at a perilous angle, causing her to pedal jerkily back and forth until she has regained equilibrium. The substantial rolls of flesh on their wobbling legs make me think of animals resiliently fleshed against harsh climes, and somehow this reassures me. I look down at my own legs, which look to me remarkably frail and vulnerable, even in blue jeans, and I suddenly worry that they'll be unable to stand up under the freight of the rest of me, carry me where I wish to go. I am also niggled by a vague sense of having left something important behind in a place I'll never have an opportunity to see again or a place that no longer exists, say in the closet of a house that's been razed. When I look back, the twins are both balanced on one foot on the seats of their unicycles, poised so steadily in a stony arabesque that it would not surprise me if streams of water were to begin to issue ornamentally from their mouths. I feel disgusted by this cheap grandstanding and resist being moved by the cheering applause around me.

Shortly before my father died, I drew a picture of the two of us standing in front of our house, waving to the viewer. Floppy-necked flowers encircled us and a moon hung low in the purple sky. My father smiled and asked where my mother was. "Is that her in the window?" he prompted.

"No," I said.

"Perhaps she's in the kitchen, out of view."

I shook my head. My father smiled. "She's dead," I said. "She's not in the house anymore."

My father stopped smiling, pinched his lips, then said, "That's not a very charitable feeling for a daughter to have toward her mother." I remember this. I remember him saying, "That's not a very charitable feeling for a daughter to have toward her mother," though the first time he said it, he reversed it: "That's not a very charitable feeling for a mother to have toward her daughter. I mean . . ." and he corrected the swap. I didn't say anything. But I thought I detected a slight note of satisfaction in his voice through his dutiful inquiry. "Don't you think you'd feel bad if your mother really were to die?"

I considered this. I had considered this before. Although I was young, I'd already experienced several deaths and so had some inkling of what was meant by the gaping absence that opened up after the casket was covered over. Once a person was there and then a person was not there, and the person not being there and not visiting you anymore or commenting on how big you were getting or how much you resembled so-and-so was the condition that seemed most likely to persist. "At first," I answered.

My father folded the picture and said, "I think we ought not to share this with your mother." I shook my head. I later made a compensatory drawing of my father and me standing in the picture window of our front room and waving to my mother as she bicycled past the house, bent over the handlebars for speed. My father looked at the picture and nodded without expression. Then I made one of my mother standing in the window, and my father and me, shrunk to size, looking at her from the open door of a small house balanced in the branches of the pin oak in our front yard. We all had flat lips and tiny eyes, but the sun sported a jagged grin. I have always wondered if my father died in order to make a point.

Time passes in a way I no longer know how to mark. I feel my bones lose density, grow brittle, imagine myself aging inside my skin at a breakneck clip, but the air around me is so still.

*   *   *

I sat on the floor in Jack's apartment. Jack was up to his elbows in clay, damp gray smeared across his naked clavicle. He sat blinking at the twisted dough of his craft, shapelessness stalled, caught in the act of turning to form. He sat with arms held up at his sides, like a surgeon waiting for gloves. In this pose, swaths of clay drying on his skin, he had the appearance of an ambivalent urn, paused between becoming and decay, held together by its contents. I imagined I could see in the mournful way Jack lowered his head the cross-purposes of body and soul and the movement of a waning resolve.

I stared out the small window, a portal that gives out onto the choppy waters of the stream of life outside. People leaned on wheelless cars propped on cinder blocks, lobbed cigarette butts at the moon; the tiny fires arced out of sight, added their light to the sky's. The lunatic moon hung there, stuck like glow-in-the-dark gum to the underside of a stadium chair, adjusting now and then its effulgent leer. Still, I was touched that it took the trouble to shine. It is bald repetition, not isolated kindness, that makes me grateful.

Clouds moved briskly overhead, began to crowd the sky, like planets congregating, and that moist star turned bilious, sick almost to doomsday with eclipse. I heard Jack washing his hands behind me.

And then I wake up and there is my father lying in bed. The age difference is not so wide now, and I touch his quiet legs. His body begins to stir and I realize it is up to me to raise him, suture his severed halves together. All eyes are on me as the halogen lights burn above us. My father is like me, hard to look at, limbs and features bent at odd angles even in repose, though reordered and fetching after the fact, when you look away and recollect, so I glance at him quickly then look at the wall and remember how beautiful he was. I kiss my father's dry lips, touch his closed eyes, and he sits up, kindled, the monster brought lovingly to life. Outside the town rumbles uncomfortably at the thought of a new creature in town; torches are lit. Will he kill the little girl? Accident or no, there will be an accounting for all missing girls.

His face colors as he works his rusty jaw, and he touches my hands, the forceps that drew him to life and lent him shape. He smiles warmly, frowns, smiles, and speaks. He calls me his little *astrum* and tells me that my careful reconstruction of history isn't entirely accurate, that I ignore salient facts and overvalue others in order to settle blame. He looks at his hands as he speaks, the reluctant revenant. Naturally, I object to this and scowl at him, sigh, wonder why resurrections always demand so much of a person. *Doesn't it mean something*, I protest, *that this is the way it occurs to me to understand my life? Doesn't that count for anything, if not truth* (as understood by one long dead, I think spitefully)? *Truth? Is that all death has done for you? Left you to police the empirical liberties I take?* I can't help heaving an audible breath of dismay. My father shakes his head, clearly weary, rubs the blue stubble of his cheek. *You died on my seventh birthday.* He nods. *You've been gone. Perhaps you've been looking on from some shelf in the universe,* I offer, *but you've not been* here.

I can see by the way my father breathes and pulls at his chin that knowing what comes after has lent him no certainty. I would like to concede to him that I feel most firm in ineffable beliefs, but fear I might lose some advantage.

You were born sick, says my father. *Breathing unsteadily, blue-bodied. Your mother . . . wasn't prepared.*

Well, it's just a feeling I have, I say, *this sense of lack, of my being alive as an impertinent excess. It's not something I can document.*

I have always worried about the irrelevance of my sorrow.

Ho-hum, this isn't it either, what I wish to say. Outside, the mob grows quiet. No lynching tonight.

My father nods regretfully. Although dead, he cannot explain it to me any better than this. There's no key, no germinal moment that will help me to understand the nature of my distortion. My father's wingtipped shoes seem so small and worn now, like the shoes of a child. The bags under his eyes sag more heavily than I remember. His skin is loose and sallow. He appears not to have gotten a good night's sleep in ages, appears deprived of essential nutrients. I wave my hands in front of him and prestidigitate him back into death.

I think to myself perhaps it is eternity I wish to rescue us from.

*　　*　　*

I don't know what I mean to anyone, and I'm tired of wondering. I don't know why the sky seems haunted by the moon. There it is again. Sometimes its constancy is irritating. I know what I said before. I think just one night without the moon—not an overcast absence but actual gap—and maybe something useful, something with the power to really exist, would fly through the lacuna it left behind. There are no offspring fires burning tonight, no small stars piggybacking. The moon is not my mother. It is not instinct or menses or augury. It is not the majestic intellect. There is no portal to my father who died on my birthday. I have wondered how a mere planet can bear all that meaning, the stories and rites, conversations and tides, and madness and metaphors it has set in motion. On clear, sleepless nights, I look up and see the bright, vigilant face hanging outside my window. It gazes down at me, swells with loneliness and longing, mourns all the other careers it might have pursued. I am not convinced that the moon I stare at is the same one Galileo ogled, or Jesus, the one that set the first wolf to howling, the same one I feared as a child. Each night with the light it sheds it becomes another moon entirely. Doffing layer after layer of light, maybe every seven years burnt new to a moon we've never known. I'm not without hope. One day it will hatch, and out of it will spring something so untenable that no myths will survive. Fat girls on high wires, men evolved to clay, blind skies forced to read the stammering braille of the lives beneath them, me lovely.

A. Wonderland

Alison is blonde and thirteen and avoids eating red meat. She once read about a man who led an art movement and demanded that his followers eat only green food because green was his favorite color. His followers complied. Alison imagines that at least these people must have gotten the recommended daily allowance of vitamin A. She has decided to name her first child, whether male or female, André after this man. She is glad that André's favorite color was not red. She thinks with a name like André, the child would be bound to excel under any circumstances. There was once a large all-star wrestler with sparse teeth and layers of fatty skin that drooped over his trunks named André the Giant. Alison hopes others will not make this association. She tries not to think about it herself.

When Alison first meets people, she sometimes tells them her last name is Wonderland. She has seen the movie *Dreamchild* four times and is disappointed each time that Lewis Carroll and young Alice do not marry in the end. She knows he's too old for Alice but feels sex with a much older man is a small price to pay for a good nonsense poem.

Alison is in class. It is a class on the Salem witch trials and the McCarthy era. It is an advanced class team-taught by Mr. Potchad and Mrs. Collins. Mr. Potchad speaks slowly and quietly and sometimes chuckles for no apparent reason, and this has earned him the nickname Mr. Pothead. Mrs. Collins has long, straight, frosted blonde hair and eats avocados every day for lunch. The class is reading *The Crucible* aloud. Alison's friend Elva Jonquil Jenkins is reading the part of Elizabeth Proctor. Alison is reading the part of Tituba, which she also considers a very nice name. Alison watches her hands shake in her lap. Her heart palpitates. She feels it miss a beat and double up on the next. She imagines a bullet of blood bouncing against her aorta. She tries to see calm pulses of blood, smooth as peeled almonds, pushing their way through her veins. She sees nothing but feels her body lifting as if she were being inhaled.

*   *   *

Alison's father takes her to the biofeedback clinic once a month, where she works on her visualization techniques. Her father was attracted to the clinic by a glossy brochure with a picture of an illuminated glass brain on the front. The brochure told the story of a young boy with an inoperable brain tumor. When conventional medicine gave him and his family no hope, they turned to the biofeedback clinic for guidance. It was the age of *Star Wars*, and the boy decided to envision his tumor as a small, round, spongy planet—Planet Meatball. Each night for fifteen minutes before he went to sleep, the boy visualized starships zooming in his brain as they destroyed Planet Meatball with their powerful lasers. One night the boy was unable to visualize this drama and could see in his mind only a tiny, white circle. The next day, the boy's doctor was thunderstruck to discover the tumor had completely disappeared, leaving behind only a small spot of calcification. Zeke, Alison's father, was very moved by this story and took Alison to the clinic the very day he received the brochure in the mail.

Alison's father is in advertising, and she was surprised at how easily he was taken in by this emotional ploy. She suspects her father has been in advertising too long. Like the actor who begins to imagine he really is living life on a riverboat after his fiftieth performance as Samuel Clemens, her father, she fears, is a little too persuaded by his own shtick, his head too easily turned by his own myths. He works for a small agency with modest accounts, hawking such products as foot powder and electrolysis. She knows he dreams of the day when he will be called on to come up with catchy lyrics like "hold the pickles, hold the lettuce." He waits for the day when he will hear people randomly humming an unshakable tune that underlies his words. Though Alison is not particularly taken with her father's line of work, she helps him with his campaigns. She came up with the tag line "Someday my prints will come" for a one-hour photomat. She has made a point, however, never to look up the word *demographics*. Alison would rather her father worked at the Roe Bowl snack bar, where a wheel of shriveled hotdogs always turns.

* * *

Elva passes Alison a note. It reads: *Darrin Maxwell gave me a Zotz in social studies today. So cool. When it sizzled in my mouth I pretended it was his tongue! Gawwwwwwwd! He told me he knows the Heimlich maneuver. I think he's HOT for me!!!* And with a single, tall S vertically connecting all the words, she pens the postscript *Sorry So Sloppy*. Alison feels heat rush up from her stomach to her cheeks.

"Tituba? Where's our Tituba?" Mrs. Collins sings.

Alison's cheeks feel hot and itch. Her head begins to throb. She sees tiny people stamping around her brain as though they were on a carnival moonwalk or as though they were snuffing out small fires. Alison pats her cheeks. She sees her heart as a metronome. She slows down the beat. The metal finger of the metronome rocks slower and slower. Her head hits her desk.

*   *   *

Alison is with Lurleen, her biofeedback counselor. Lurleen has a long, thick rope of braided, blonde hair, and pink plastic cat glasses. She wears perfumed oil called "China Rain." She is missing the top part of her left ear; she told Alison how it blackened and fell off one winter like a seasonal antler. It had become frostbitten at a bus stop during a winter storm. In the top of her other ear, she has a tiny gold stud.

Alison is thinking about her mother, Glenda. Glenda left when Alison was seven. The day before Glenda left, she dressed Alison up. She braided her fine hair and coiled and pinned the woven pigtails to the sides of her head. "Looks like lumpy snails," Alison had said.

"It does not," Glenda said. "It's nice."

Alison raised her arms in the air, and Glenda dropped the white eyelet dress neatly over Alison's head, as though she were covering a toaster. Glenda slipped pink anklets over Alison's feet, small and smooth as decorative soaps. Alison stepped into black patent-leather shoes. As Glenda clipped pearl pendant earrings onto Alison's tiny lobes, Alison rocked back and forth and sang. "Have you ever ever ever in your long-legged life . . ."

"Alison, hold still."

"Call me Jot."

"I will not. Alison is a perfectly nice name."

Alison fingered her ears. "My teacher, Mrs. Nilsson, said that large ears like mine are a sign of good health."

"What?"

Zeke walked into the room. "Hey, Jot. You're not ready for Brownies," he said.

"Her name is Alison, and she's not going to Girl Scouts this week."

"But they're churning butter today, and she's been looking forward to it all week, haven't you, Pumpkin?"

Alison looked at her shoes. Glenda snapped the earrings from her lobes. "Go then and pick up worse habits."

Alison held her hands over her ears. "I'm a child," she said.

Lurleen hugs a clipboard to her chest. "So what do you think happened?"

"My blood pressure dropped, I guess, and I fainted."

"Still not able to control those negative pictures?"

"I tried. They come from someplace outside and fly into my thoughts like, like evil birds." Alison rubs her temples. *Sacred*, she is thinking.

"Now, see there. That's a negative metaphor." Lurleen grabs Alison's hand.

"Simile." Alison touches the earring in Lurleen's ear. "Did that hurt?"

"Just cartilage," she says. "I saw it as the final puzzle piece, and it was as if the hole was already there. The lady that did it said, 'This can cause arthritis, you know,' and I said, 'Yeah, well I don't plan on doing any heavy lifting with this ear anyway.'" Lurleen laughs and her big, yellow teeth remind Alison of kitchen tiles whose color would be called Harvest. "How are the palpitations?" Lurleen pats her own chest.

Alison feels her heart skipping. "They're still there," she says.

"And the ears?"

"Still there."

*　*　*

Alison remembers being a small child. She felt very small. She often imagined she was something her mother had bought for a quarter out of one of those machines in the entrance of a Kmart. Something that came folded in a small, lidded, plastic ball. Something like a rain bonnet or a slender watch that said 12:15 from one angle, 6:30 from another. Glenda was nervous around her. She was afraid Alison's childhood wasn't going well. She would sit and watch her play, and if Alison would look up, she'd say, "What? What do you mean?" and Alison would walk over to her and pet her hand.

They frequently ate fish sticks and canned cranberry sauce that was borne into the dish in the perfect shape of the can, round and ribbed and flat on the ends. Glenda would ask, "Is this right? Is this enough?" Alison would reply, "There needs to be broccoli and chocolate cake," or "We've forgotten the butter beans and the Apple Brown Betty." At these times Glenda would look at Alison with the frozen, startled expression of a jacklighted animal.

Alison knows she cannot remember her birth and hospital stay, but sometimes she ignores what is likely and convinces herself she can. She sees a palsied body covered with light-blue skin. She feels the uncertain flow of blood through her infant veins, narrow and fragile as fiber-optic threads. She feels her head swell and shrink, her soft spot stretch and pucker. She feels her heart, no bigger than a kidney bean, pop and swallow. Warm threads of blood slip from her ears and pool near her tiny nape. A transparent dome surrounds her, as though she were the main course of an expensive meal. She sees the empty, transparent rubber gloves reaching through portholes in the dome and lying lifeless beside her. She feels her legs twitch and snap. Alison opens her eyes and sits up. She touches the blood on her pillow. She puts her fingers in her ears. She imagines herself recounting this experience to Lurleen, Lurleen saying, "You're doing this to yourself, you know. Psychosomatic. You're digressing again," Alison responding, "Re. Regressing."

*　*　*

It is evening and Alison is sitting at a TV tray, eating a TV dinner, watching the evening news. Her dinner consists of beef bordeaux, glazed carrots with pearl onions, herb noodles, and a small gummy square of bread pudding. Her father asked her to try it to see if she could think of a fresh approach. It is currently being pitched as lo-cal, semi-gourmet, "fast food" (it is microwaveable), but sales are down.

Alison places two pearl onions on the canvas of beef. She completes the face with a mouth of carrot. She thinks, *It's all in the presentation.* She stares at the food face, into the pupilless eyes. She imagines herself a tiny onion, layer upon layer of intricate skin, wrapped in herself, never opening voluntarily, never blooming. She rests at the cool bottom of someone's martini. She sits, unblinking, atop someone's slice of beef bordeaux.

"Earth to Alison. Come in Alison." Zeke waves a hand in front of his daughter's glazed eyes. "Hello? Anybody in there? Well, I see you haven't outgrown playing with your food."

"No one else will play with me," she says.

"Ha, ha." Zeke picks up one of the onion eyes and pops it into his mouth. "Say, are you mad because I don't like to play Scrabble with you anymore? You always win anyway, so what's the point? It's redundant. You're the lexical queen—I concede." Zeke pushes the onion into his cheek, as though it were a jawbreaker.

"You've blinded it." Alison pushes the other onion eye to the center of the imaginary brow. "Doomed to Cyclops," she says.

Zeke picks up a carrot and smells it. "So, how is it? Have you tried any of it yet?"

"Better than Lincoln Logs, but it doesn't hold a candle to Lean Cuisine," Alison says. "And it certainly isn't fish sticks and cranberry sauce."

On the news, the mass murderer Ted Bundy talks to a reporter. He is awaiting his execution. He tells the reporter that pornography worked him into a frenzy, inciting him to commit his diabolical crimes. He says he has other murdering friends and acquaintances and they all agree that pornography is the instigator. The picture switches to a shot of the enormous crowd of people gathered outside the prison. People are cheering and chanting and laughing. Children ride atop the shoulders of their parents and clap their hands above their heads. One man proudly pulls his T-shirt taut so the glittery letters that spell out the words *Burn Bundy Burn* can be easily seen as a camera pans across the crowd. Twenty seconds before the switch is to be flipped, before the current is to bubble through the convicted man's veins, the crowd begins to count down. "20, 19, 18, 17 . . . 4, 3, 2, 1." The crowd explodes with sound and movement, as if it too were wired. Fireworks and noisemakers sound, confetti and streamers blind the cameras. A man wearing glasses with springy, drooping eyeballs capers in front of a camera. Alison feels her mouth begin to water and runs to the bathroom.

Alison remembers her mother's leaving. Her mother's hand shook as she smoked a cigarette, sprinkling ashes on the carpet. She positioned Alison on the divan and kneeled in front of her. She put her cigarette out and clutched both of Alison's hands. "I have to go away, Alison," she said. "It will be the best thing all around. I'm just not very good at this mother stuff. You know that."

"You're okay," Alison said. "You forget things sometimes."

Glenda clutched her own arms as she stood up. "I'm not good

at it. You make me nervous and Zeke makes me nervous, and I'm no good at putting Mercurochrome on your sores. I'm not good at making your hair look nice or reading stories with the right whimsical inflection. We have nothing in common."

Alison walked to her mother and held her hand. Glenda pulled her hand away and held it to her chest. "I don't like to be touched.

"I'm sorry," she said, picking up her suitcases. "It's just not working out." Glenda stared out the screen door. "Perhaps I can't forgive you and your father for the pain of childbirth. I was in labor for nearly two days, and then after all that, you weighed only four pounds." Glenda laughed. She bent over and lifted one of Alison's braids to her mouth and kissed it.

As soon as Glenda was out the door, Alison's father jumped into the room and yelled, "Surprise!" He was wearing a party hat and shaking maracas. "La cucaracha! La cucaracha! Come on, Ali, we're going to celebrate. No room for gloom here. She's dead to us, Al. D-E-A-D, dead. We're going to celebrate our independence. What do you say?" He lifted Alison onto his shoes and sambaed around the room. They spun in circles. Alison went limp as her heart beat irregularly. Blood slipped from her left ear and trailed down her neck.

Alison sits in front of the toilet, her heart and mind racing. She wishes her hair were still long enough to braid. She wishes her favorite television program, *This Old House*, were on. She thinks Bob Vila is kind and wise. She is soothed by the constant activity, the measuring, drilling, caulking. She is amazed how walls always turn out as planned, bathtubs always fit.

Alison is looking at her mother's distorted profile through the peephole in the front door. She thinks if people who don't like the way they look could see themselves through peepholes, which erase all traces of beauty from everyone, they wouldn't feel so bad. Her mother's face balloons like a hallucination as she moves closer and narrows to a pinpoint as she moves back.

Since she left, Glenda has called Alison several times to wish her a happy birthday, though she was usually off by three or four weeks. Once she had a local florist send Alison an exotic plant, whose fronds of leaves would close like secretive, green jaws when touched. The card said, *Sometimes I wish you were here*, but didn't say where *here* was.

Alison opens the door. Her mother has long blondish-white hair that is ponytailed. She is wearing a denim jacket, a black knee-length skirt that fits like a bandage, white crew socks, and pink Converse high-tops. On the lapel of the denim jacket is a button that says, *Walk Stickly and Carry a Big Soft*. Alison notices the fine, upward-stretching lines around her mother's eyes and wonders what she's been smiling or squinting at. Glenda steps toward Alison then backs up and extends her hand.

"Hello," she says. Alison shakes her hand. Glenda enters and walks into the living room, seating herself on the divan. Alison sits on the floor across from her. "I know it's not your birthday," Glenda says, laughing.

"No, but you're closer than usual," Alison says. "Only two weeks away."

"Really? Pure coincidence."

Alison remembers the time the brakes went out on her bicycle as she flew down the steep hill of Forty-ninth Street. She wore out the soles of her tennis shoes trying to slow down and ended up careening into a ditch to stop. She dislocated her shoulder and the cartilage cushioning her jaw slipped around the mandibular bone, wedged itself behind the joint, and prevented her from opening her mouth more than a sliver. When she told her mother, through clenched teeth, what had happened, her mother replied, "Why weren't you playing piano? You should have been playing the piano."

"We don't have a piano," Alison said.

"Well, if you'd been looking for a piano to play, this never would have happened."

"It was an accident," Alison said.

"There are no accidents," Glenda replied. "I suppose now we'll have to get you those new Day-Glo tennis shoes you've been harping about." Then Glenda bit into the back of her hand until it bled and said, "Those weren't the right things to say, were they?"

Glenda reaches into the pocket of her denim jacket and pulls out a cassette tape and a clear plastic bracelet filled with pastel beads. "Here," she says. Alison takes the tape and bracelet from her. "It's candy," Glenda says. Alison looks at the cassette. "I mean the bracelet. The beads inside the bracelet."

"I don't eat very much sugar," Alison says.

"Guess you don't take after me."

"No."

"You like the Bulgarian Women's Choir?" Glenda asks.

"I don't know."

Alison is afraid Glenda has X-ray eyes. She knows it is not possible, but something about the way Glenda is staring right at her makes her feel as if she is being cut open. The skin and muscle are pulled back in a wide grin. Her rib cage is pried easily open like the hinged wooden purses her grandmother used to carry. Glenda is fingering her heart, poking at the rubbery red matter as though it were only a meringue that refused to peak, stroking the glass-smooth ventricles. Alison knows Glenda sees the even clicking of blood. She sees her mother's eyes move up, out of the heart. They crawl up the spine, behind her esophagus, perching on brain stem. She feels her mother's eyes staring at the gray cauliflower, eyeing pockets of lies and deceit.

"Did you hear me?" Glenda asks. "I said I went to Kansas City. Sort of on a lark. You know what? They have this giant statue of Alfred E. Newman in the parking lot of this filling station. Pretty wild. That's not why I went of course. Delta was offering round-trip tickets for sixty-five bucks.

"I went to the American Royal there. It's sort of a glorified indoor rodeo. I wasn't really sure what to expect, but they had calf roping, and I can't really stomach calf roping, so I left and went to this bar. I met the strangest kid there. He had the most beautiful hands I've ever seen. He was the singer for the house band. His name was Clancy, and his brown hair stood straight up in the air like a sun-scorched lawn. You ought to do something fun with your hair."

"We often go bowling together."

Glenda laughs but stops short. Alison stands up. "Can I get you a beverage?"

"A beverage? What kind of word is that, beverage? I must have missed more of your birthdays than I thought."

"We have Perrier, Sleepytime and Red Zinger tea, grape juice, and Dr. Pepper." Alison sees her mother staring at her again and covers her chest with both hands as if to prevent something from leaping out.

"Didn't they just recall Perrier because they found benzene in some of it?"

"Yes, but that wasn't ours. Do you want something or not?"

"Not." Glenda stands and moves toward Alison. Alison moves to one side as if to let her pass.

Alison remembers her great grandma Reese, her mother's grandmother, who always kept Kleenex tucked beneath her watchband. When she was eighty-two, she had to have a pin put in her hip, and forever after she was frightened of metal objects because she thought they might secretly be magnetized. She was afraid the objects would suck her toward them and seize her, never let her go. She abandoned her watch. She was particularly frightened of the radiator. She took to eating only dried fruit, which she believed had a neutralizing effect on the magnetism.

"Should we do something?" Glenda asks, taking a step backward.

"Like what?" Alison stares at her mother's tanned forearms, the fine white mist of hair that covers them. She wonders what she was doing at the time her mother was cultivating this tan, at the time bursts of melanin were blooming beneath her mother's skin. In math class, she thinks, examining the even beauty of an isosceles triangle or drawing huge dinosaur humps with the inside of her protractor, not even considering the fact that someone she knew was lying on a lawn chair somewhere, drinking sun tea, listening to a top forty countdown, and absorbing the color-altering heat of the sun. Alison is amazed how so much can happen without your knowledge, leaving you with only aftereffects and inferences.

"I don't know. Would you like a new pair of shoes?" Glenda twists and rubs her fingers.

"I'd better stay here. Does Dad know you're here?"

"No. I didn't even know I was coming until this morning."

"We could watch television."

"All right."

Alison and Glenda sit on the divan. Alison fishes the remote control from beneath one of the cushions. She turns on the television. "We missed *Jeopardy* and *A Current Affair*," she says. She changes the channel to the public television station. A nature special entitled *Termites of Endearment* is just starting.

"Yuck," Glenda says.

"This is a good one. I've seen it before. It's about how some termites sacrifice themselves for the advancement of the rest of the colony."

"Those would be the ones in the Debra Winger role, I guess." Glenda laughs. Alison does not.

Alison presses the mute button. "Do you remember in second grade when I gave Jason Ordway an Alka-Seltzer and told him it was a new kind of candy? Then after he ate it, I told him he should wash it down with a big drink of water, and he did, and he got sick and said his heart hurt. I got sent home, and you told me that now I was always going to have to look over my shoulder because things like that come back to haunt you, and I got dehydrated because I was afraid to drink water."

"Why do you always bring these things up, Alison? If anything, surely they must justify my leaving." Glenda stands up. "I wasn't trying to be abusive or malicious, I was just in the wrong role. It's like someone who yearns to be a baker trying to be a cardiologist or something just because it's expected of them."

"I'm not a blintz," Alison says. "No one's life is altered when someone decides not to make donuts. I have palpitations."

Glenda picks up Alison's eighth grade school picture off the coffee table. She kisses it, sets it down, smiles at Alison, and leaves.

Alison looks at the bowed, convex world outside the peephole. "The Sound and the Sound," she says, "by Alison Wonderland. Skimming the spilt milk with flatulent flair, and guarding the old bard to boot, kicking the cat with cacophonous care, spleens shiver shards hither and nod. Stop with a start Saint Ignatius pig lips, beginning with in the beguine, crackle pop snaps parsimonious snips, while bladderfowl create a scene. Thank you." She bows. "Thank you all." Alison feels her body begin to slip out from under her. She tries to corral her senses. She thinks of school.

Ancient Egyptians. Yesterday in humanities class, she read about small statues called *kas* that were considered receptacles for the soul. When important people died, they were placed inside tombs full of food and jewels, beside their own personalized *kas*. These statues acted, they believed, as turnstiles between this world and the next, allowing their souls to escape their bodies and pass on to the afterlife. "Better safe than sorry," Alison says.

Alison feels dizzy. She feels as though she were at the bottom of a malt beneath a straw or buried in a tangle of shag carpeting under the rumble and whir of a vacuum, as if she were being sucked out of this world. "My heartbeat is calm and regular," she whispers to herself. "My breathing is slow and even." She removes the barrette decorated with worry dolls from her hair. She holds it next to her temple, closes her eyes. She is unable to imagine what anything looks like. She sees only circles of light.

Cassandra Mouth

1. *Never Trust an Animal that Appears Suddenly*

It was a day painful with sunshine when I said *Dog* and one appeared in my garden, lumbering out of the foliage like time-lapse botanical evolution, plant to animal in a matter of minutes, the time it takes to name the outcome of a foregone conclusion. It was a mastiff ropy with brawn, weaving in a way that said it was spoiling for a scrap with an obsequious lap dog. I knelt to claim it, be claimed by it, held out my hand, smaller than its paws. It sniffed the grass then wagged its sculpted haunches, loped toward me. I imagined its slobbering muzzle buried gratefully in my palm, its skin shivering with the satisfaction of encountering a beneficent creature with an endless supply of bone-shaped food in her cupboard. As it came toward me, I saw its heavy testicles swinging, that lightly furred, leathery sack of canine perpetuity, and I saw the progeny in his future, wormy thug pups that would force their eyes open prematurely, develop a menacing gait. Then he trotted past me, gaze forward, wagged his way to the woman standing behind me in the street, a woman wearing dark glasses, a flowered sundress and yellow hat, skin so tan she seemed purple. She knelt, held out her hand.

So is it always. Though I can predict it, I make myself blind with hope I know is fated to be dashed, an impotent optimism I know will one day erase me. I am a collection of faint pencil strokes on onionskin, a script that blurs imperceptibly with daily handling, fading in the sebum of more definitive fingers.

2. Don't Rely on Augury to Know When to Wear a Parka

When my mother calls to tell me the weather is soon to turn, though it's early, to tell me to take my sweaters out of the cedar chest, I tell her I know, the mercury will drop this very night, plummet below freezing, causing porch plants to shrivel with hypothermic shock. Tomorrow, TV meteorologists will distract viewers from the previous night's inaccurate forecast by capering on camera in mittens and parkas. I wonder, says my mother, if I should bring in my begonias. Your flowers will die, I say, go limp, translucent, blooms and stems withering, the thick leaves of your jade plant falling off like frostbitten toes. I think I'll wait, she says. The drop will be gradual. The season is so short. I'll give them another day to soak up the final drizzle of sunshine. I see the clay pots full of dry dirt and old roots that will line her porch through the winter.

3. Dreaming Will Only Make You Hoarse

I dream myself, underwater, keening at a glass surface, my diluted voice not even conjuring bubbles, sound lodged somewhere in my sternum.

4. Is That a Tumor in Your Brain or Are You Happy to See God?

At work, as I place the lead vest over shoulders, drape it across laps, I try not to see the burgeoning tumors, the wayward cells colonizing the native putty of being. I know it's an invasion, peering into the crystal ball of the body, eyeing its eventualities, but my eyes stare into portent even when closed. I touch the dark spots on the spectral record of the body's interior, touch the dim fissures and opaque intimations. Once I passed a child on her way to an MRI, a tumor the size of a hazelnut bullying its way into her brainstem. My face tensed when I saw it, and the child stopped and patted me on the arm. "God is love?" she asked, squinting as if adjusting to sudden sunlight. "Love is blind," I returned, determined to liberate us both from illusions. We pictured a fiercely scowling, milky-eyed man, rag-tag and smelling of urine, holding out a cup in a fiery hand, the word FORGIVE-NESS stamped in the tin. Humans, the mundane braille that God fingers when he needs to find a flophouse, weary from all the begging.

5. One Man's Hearing is Another's Impairment

My lover listens with the aid of a device, pink and coiled like a tiny fetus resting inside his ear. It is dark in his room, but I see his eyes going dim like the screen of an old Philco TV reducing itself to a silver horizon, a luminous dot. I am here, I say. Where are you? he asks. I put my mouth to his belly, bite. Touch me here, he says, pointing to the imprint of my teeth. I circle my tongue around his chin. Your mouth here, he says, touching the delicate cleft. I take the hearing aid from his ear, put my lips to the cavity and blow. He hears, says, Fortuity, Embezzlement, Disappearance, Metastasis.

6. From Your Mouth to God's Hand

In his front room is a round table covered with a black and purple cloth batiked with owls. I sit beneath the table and trace my finger along the backside of the cloth, the horned tufts that crown the owls' heads. There is a knock, and my lover lets his client in. The woman sits down at the table, and feet in brown suede pumps appear, neatly parallel, on the floor behind me. The ankles are thin and the bones press through the tops of the feet, a trellis draped in skin. My lover removes his hearing aid, birthing his deafness, passes the device under the table to me. I hear the static that roars inside his ear, the white noise of prophecy. People place stock in the physical impediments of oracles, believe congenital vexation of the body must be compensated, must result in sensitivity to extrasensory rumblings. My lover's spirit, they imagine, is horn-shaped, amplifying the inscrutable godvoice that hums inaudibly beneath the surface.

With one hand, my lover holds the wrist of his client. He offers the other hand to me under the table. I press my lips to his palm and mouth the woman's future into his skin. He tells her she should move to the desert, where life springs green and spiny through small cracks in adversity. He tells her that erasing the body will not save the soul, that she should not see flesh as an iron-mawed trap she must gnaw herself free of.

The feet disappear from beneath the table, but I continue to hold my lover's hand to my mouth. He turns his hand over and takes my wrist. I put my other hand to my mouth, feel the velvety movement of my lips against my palm. I see my skin grow sheer, hear my voice turn to wind.

7. If You Can Read This, You're Too Close

My eyes are ponderous with sight, eyelids drooping like window shades with weighted pulls. The people who seek answers from my lover can barely keep their eyes in their heads, eyeballs empty, transparent, buoyant as effervescence.

The cross that stoops the back of the prophet is her own conclusion, the film of her departure projected interminably on the screen of her eyes. What I have always seen, in the moments when I'm left utterly alone, is my own unmaking, cells loosening, life moving backward from two legs to four to the scaly arc and rudder of prehistory and the phosphorescent shimmer before that, to the dissonant whir of life plotting its inception, from dry land to water to improbable inkling, the body devolved, a life unauthored.

My voice vibrates in the ears of the unsuspecting; the familiar timbre makes them tug at their earlobes, the sound of belated intuition. My lips, forever parted, the very shape of vanity. Those who seek credit for foresight sport ample, pouty lips, mouths that suggest they fancy themselves on speaking terms with deities.

Every mouth is entitled to only so many words, every page too. The mouth and pencil at rest are things to be lauded. Physics tells us we are the prediction of what happens elsewhere. Let the elsewhere begin. In the end, I breathe into my hand, watch with the wary eyes and elevated pulse of a tornado tracker, with a body tilted happily toward disaster, as the unheeded mouth closes, as a fine script disappears from a page, fading with each preoccupied reading, letters seeming to lift off the page as they whiten.

Swallowing Angels Whole

I bought a little tent, a poor little tent very full of holes,
and from that I saved my money and bought a bigger one,
and that has been the history.

AIMEE SEMPLE McPHERSON

In the beginning, there was the Word, and the word was me, and I was a baby. As I got older, I saw there were others, but still I suspected it was all about me. It wasn't until I realized that I might be the other myself that I began to feel a vague discomfort, like a hand-me-down sweater a size too small. One day at Sunday school, looming in the dusty night sky of the chalkboard was a giant white eye, unblinking. White lashes, white pupil, and outline of iris, it was upsetting. "God sees you," said the teacher. Whereas before I had comfortably imagined myself floating in the eyes of everyone, suddenly I craved invisibility.

To my mother, on the ride home, I said, "Surely, he cannot see us in here, through the hood of the buggy?" My mother looked me squarely in the eyes, her needlepoint stare causing them to water, and said, "He can." At home, in the wooden bin among potatoes and onions, I called out, "And now?" My mother thumped the lid and pronounced: "No escape."

My mother had told me I am Love, it is my name—Aimee—and when I espied men furtively cupping the faces of women in their hands, I understood that I was the blood rush of heat that pinked those cheeks. Tucked in the middle of my name like a stubborn egg inside a hen was a me I could not suffer anyone hatching, least of all a God who craftily hid in every pocket of Being, whose mug was writ too wide to see. *The aim is me, the aim is me, the aim is me!* I incanted.

I felt that cold, white eye on me as I twitched my nose, tapped my foot, felt it recording my every move. I could barely breathe beneath its ceaseless observation. At night I undressed under blankets but felt the stare on my skin sure as a rash as the wool prickled against my stomach and legs. Then one night, beneath the covers, in double darkness, I told myself a story. I said, *There was a little girl who grew up bigger than God, big, so big God couldn't keep His eye on all of her, and when the people saw how big she was, they clapped and tossed her chocolate coins, then she shrank to the size of a mite, small small small, and leapt inside God's eye. Safely on the other side of His vision, she jumped in the air and grabbed God's frozen eyelid then pulled it shut like a window shade.*

It was then that I got an inkling of how I might tell myself a story and lose myself in the words that made me up, and how I might slowly take a shape inside that loss.

Truth is what you get when you let yourself know nothing, really know it. It's as absolute as a dark hole whose bottom cannot be experienced except in faith and dreams. And that's the story. The real story.

Silver eyes and lips in the water, my face floating and voice returning to me, my face and rippled skin, no sun, and skin, in the water, my voice speaks to me and I want to meet, my voice speaks, it repeats my words, I follow and I am a child, the voice repeats, the hair falls forward, want to touch her, she knows me, I will fill the pail with myself, my face in the water, she speaks so clearly, I can lower myself into her, into the moving outline of her face, into the soft voice generous as an open hand, the shifting outline the voice moves through, I will lower myself into the beautiful voice, into the mouth, the black circle calling me.

Like that.

This is a story.

I was a little girl, young. I climbed up on the well and saw her. She called me, the little girl in the well. We had chickens and goats and cows and dogs, and now there was a little girl whose face flowered in the water. Her voice was beautiful, like ice breaking on the river. I loved her, of course.

I loved my first husband, Robert. His God-words burned me and my own voice bubbled from the wounds. My whole body spoke; it stuttered and screamed. My limbs flailed with belief.

I would follow him to the other side of the world to gather souls. When I was a child, I tried to dig through the ground to a place I'd seen in picture books, a place where people wore straw hats as big as mixing bowls, upside down, on their heads. Now I would travel there with purpose. I would follow and Robert would end there, his seed stashed inside me.

It was the arithmetic of belief that originally appealed to me, the repetitions that persuade by brute accumulation like the ticking of a clock you ignore until late at night when it clicks in your ear undeniably and you realize your sleep has been keeping time to the sound; it has hummed in your ear while you slept. I was a sensible girl. *There are twenty times as many references to His coming with a crown, honored and worshipped by all the ends of the earth, as to His coming with a cross, and being wounded in the house of His friends. In the 260 chapters of the New Testament, the second coming of Jesus Christ is definitely referred to 318 times.* One out of every thirty verses, voilá, Jesus Christ redux. *The Epistles of Paul, while referring to water baptism only 13 times, refer to the second coming 50 times,* which, according to my calculations, provides one hundred opportunities to up the ante on faith (the first coming, came?, implicit, you see, in the return). And there it is. That's belief. The square root of salvation: our Lord and Savior. He came once, he'll come again. But these were the idle doodles of a restless schoolgirl. Genuine enlightenment would not turn the gas up on my dim thoughts until I heard Robert's voice, a voice I had heard in my dreams.

And then I had to let go the innocent heresy of science. In school, I thrilled to discussions of Darwin's theories and wondered if he had felt the walk out of the water into the light click in his own bones, the weight of that forward movement pressing down on his skeleton. Bones remember. The ache that starts at the base of the spine is a bone memory of another posture. But once Robert's hot words crackled across my skin and into my small, gray heart, there was no room for natural selection in my spiritual evolution. Suppose faith were to be selected out. What would I be left with? Malingering phantom stirrings of gills and a prehensile tail? Suffer those of us interested in invisible origins.

Nineteen ten, a decade après de siècle, the apocalyptic approach of which I was too young to fear, Hong Kong, fragrant harbor, in the hills above Wanchai in the summer, there was rebellion in the air. You could hear it in the sizzle of mosquitoes. It eventually raged through my Robert's body. I watched funeral processions march through the thick stew of humidity into the cemetery our house adjoined. Bodies twisted and curled in the flames of the pyres. The black smoke rose without distinction.

Who speaks this? you wonder. I wonder. I am rupture, all gap, space elbowed between pieces once intimate. This voice crawls out of my mouth like so many insects buzzing, a foreign sound, like water dripping in a tin cup, small and hollow. I want to be pure, empty. My true voice is the one heard by the girl in the well. The voice I use to speak to God, frilled with a tremulous piety even when I sit in the closet and pray, is not my real voice.

The voice that will settle inside me rings in a register only the ghosts of the living can hear. That's who will come to the tents and the temple. Spirits will part the heavy flesh and it is to them I will address the Word. I will see the ghosts dangle and clink like acoustic shingles hung from the ceiling to help my message resonate more clearly. The bodies below will slump and shake with affect, but it is only their own organs and arteries ticking away. They cannot escape the thump of the pulse in their ears.

These bodies and attendant souls will not be drawn by notoriety, by the tongues of flame of my oratory, curled back and forth like a beckoning finger, but by the fragile hum of vowels that lodge in my throat as I sit in my study before the sermon and rock on my knees and see nothing.

In Macao I screamed, my womb wandered, the pink-bellied worms in buckets, black-winged sampans always bobbing on the water, worms held above eager mouths, my face drawn and Robert green and thin; my eyes ached and the heat crawled inside me and fell asleep and still I was cold. With a neighborly clicking of my tongue, I befriended the rats as they scurried past, and little ghosts welled before me, stringy with heat, and Robert's face the color of cooked cabbage, my womb, weary, settled to sleep in the bounce of a jinriksha and moved away from me toward the molten crowds of Kowloon, the dogs and eggs and the souls unsaved. The rats left too, rubbing sickness from their whiskers, and the amah cried on the other side of the netting; parasols spun in the sunlight as I lay in a soup of sweat and feces.

God was wise to hide Himself from the stench and unholy rolling of our bodies.

There is nothing mystical in shit. Bodies are most themselves when they are immersed in the effluvium of their own potential.

My dream broke with my fever in Matilda Hospital. My body was barely a body, so thin and weak. I was widowed, abroad, a child on the way. I hadn't the strength to tremble. The doctors said it was the vegetables fertilized with human excrement that claimed Robert's life.

Everyone loved Robert, his careful eyes, forgiving lips. He listened intently to any confession, any quandary, and I always felt as though it was his devoted attention, a healing poultice, that drew my words to the surface. I think God was lonely for a sympathetic ear.

Here is a story I tell myself when I am tired: *Once when I was a child in Ontario, I walked through a thick enclosure of trees and stopped when I heard a rustling behind me. As I turned around, I saw a bear, who saw me and rose up on the black barrels of his legs. A growl thundered from deep in his chest and he lifted his arms. I dropped to my knees and curled into myself, a trembling hedgehog. I heard the bear grunt and lumber toward me, and I felt the smack of his paw on my back. Silently, I begged Jesus to call the bear away. And then I felt the bear's hot body cover me. The bear stretched himself over me, fitted himself to me like a hat to a head, and dug into the earth near my knees. I felt his rough tongue moving across my neck and hands. The weight of him made my body ache and feel as if it were shrinking into a flattened pebble of bone and flesh. Then the bear nuzzled his snout against my head and pried my arm loose. He pushed his clammy nose into my ear. His breath was hot and smelled of fish, and his breathing rattled like something had come loose inside him. I felt his haunches tighten against my backside, and the bear whispered, "Jesus loves you," a sentiment he sealed by lapping my ear with his sticky tongue, as if to cleanse it*

of all the uncertainties it had heard. Then the great weight of the
bear lifted, and I heard sticks snap as he left me, small and scared,
among the trees.

There are those who will say, Could this not have been one of
Satan's disguises? To which I will respond, No, for I have always
been stronger than Satan; even as a little girl I could throw him
from my back just by breathing deep.

After five months, I returned from Hong Kong, with losses and
gains disproportionate. I had lost my husband, saved scant souls,
and given birth to a sickly infant. God's ways troubled me and
left me feeling weak, dispirited, empty of offerings.

My mother took Baby Roberta to live with her. "You must heal
your wounds and find your way," she said. Time passed slowly, as
it does when you're watching.

I moved to the States and eventually found temporary comfort
in the strong arms of another, but my days in Rhode Island could
not be said to have been providential for either Harold McPherson
or me. Though I adopted his name, I never quite warmed to the
life it carried with it. A second pregnancy quickly followed. The
swell of myself gave me something to stare at and smooth, a place
to settle my restless hands, hands whose unconscious longing to
caress the hot cheeks of the hungry could be seen in the way
they floated in the air toward nothing. But after Rolf was safely
delivered into the world, I drew away from that world, into the
empty heat inside me; I curled into the blood-soft space they
would eventually cut away.

Harold was as practical as soap. It was clear to him that I was
broken and he sent for doctors to mend me. The sleeping and
crying and praying, fasting and compulsive cleaning had left my
hair sprung and wandering, knotted in spots, and my skin hung
on me like an old robe, loose and yellow. My eyes were circles of
mud sunk deep in my face. My chin was crusted with dried saliva.
I didn't fight it. Inside I was clean and combed and smelled of

anise. I looked out at those shaking heads and thought, *You can have the outside, this wretched carapace. You can carve it up and feed it to pigs if you like.*

There were many operations: bright lights and white masks, white bodies and green walls, knives and needles, and they took away parts of me I was no longer attached to; they cut and things fell away. They thought, *Maybe the sickness lives here,* Harold's head shaking with each new failure, knives flashing like sharp metal teeth; blood blooming on starched aprons reminded me of the little white dress with red moons I wore as a child, and I could have told them that when they were finished shearing off bits of disease, I'd be no bigger than a fig or an egg, something Harold could hide in his pocket, yet those clouds of covered faces continued to collect above me, and they trimmed and clamped until they hoisted me out of myself—they popped the crumbling yoke of me out of the carved cup where I hid.

They called it hysteria, an unpleasant condition common to women whose wombs get too restless and cause trouble for others. These strong-willed pouches, when they are empty, get a wild hair and itch for life that can only be found elsewhere, always elsewhere. Perhaps they're only looking for a reason not to wander, but they're always corralled in the end, put down like feral dogs.

The cure for hysteria is hysterectomy—pluck the offender from the unwitting vessel. As you can see, language corroborates this choice of treatment.

I died, or almost. In the final swoon, I looked down at the thatch of fresh scars (to this day I have difficulty gauging the whims of my bladder) and God's voice said—with the same hot insistence of the bear's—*Eternity's just around the corner. Don't rush it. Go and do the work.* So I sat up. I left my husband. I bought a car.

You end, begin. You continue.

My instincts told me to start at the beginning (as unreliable as I now know this to be), so I returned home to Ontario and in Mount

Forest, I drew my first crowd. I dragged a chair to the middle of town one morning and stood on it, stiff and straight, and faced the sky, arms reaching toward the blue flaps visible through the torn bandage of clouds. I stared into the air; birds and insects populated my gaze. Throughout the morning, clouds crowded my view, swam through the sky where my eyes locked. I imagined God looking down at the fraying white backsides of clouds whose bellies I tracked for hours. My body felt tight and pointed; my arms ached, but my aim was sure, and the shuffling of voices and feet around me sent a tingle up my shins, up and up and straight to my fingers. The current of the crowd moved through me into the atmosphere and rivaled the clouds in altitude. It bubbled upward through the spheres on an arrow course for Jesus, and when it reached him, I saw it clearly, it stood his hair on end as though he'd rubbed his head with a balloon.

Someone touched me, testing for catalepsy, and I leapt from the chair and said, "Follow me, quick!" They ran behind me and like a dam breaking they poured into the Victory Mission, where, before the day was through, every last tongue wagged indecipherably in the dialect of angels, and bodies rumbled and fizzed, infused with the Holy Spirit. When the Spirit swept through a crowd, you could feel it start slow in the ground beneath your feet, barely a shiver, until the whole building reverberated with proof of faith, bodies quaking and rolling like coins in the Sunday plate.

When it was over, when all the souls were safely stored in God's pocket, all I could clearly remember were those clouds connecting His eyes to mine.

That night, Robert came to me as I knelt down beside my bed. His auburn hair was wavier than I remembered. His pallor was certainly that of a ghost, though it was hard to say because he'd always been wan. He knelt beside me and took my hands in his. I felt almost swarthy next to him, sepia-tinted, earth to his air, the divide between proof and faith. His face was much fuller than the picture of him I carried in my head, a shifting composite from the months in China. His days in Heaven seemed to have agreed with him.

He placed his hands on my waist and turned me, drew me to him. He placed his cheek next to mine and I felt moist heat dampen my skin. He whispered in tongues in my ear, syllables snapping, the harsh crack of k's, the throaty warble of r's, and a roiling soak of vowels. I felt it deep in the gutted land between my legs. Then he licked my lips and disappeared. I pulled my lips into my mouth and sucked on them through the night and into dreams.

Do I win you? Which words do you pass on, which ones ingest? And chronology, does it lend credibility? *Jesus Christ is the same today, yesterday, and forever.*

The healing began accidentally as, I suppose, most genuinely divine things do, or so it would seem to us. I'm sure human chance and fortuity are written in God's design. Monkey Abe was the man in our town who was the receptacle for people's pent-up, boiling-point anger, held in during long and silent winter months. When folks finally regained their voices, able to speak freely without their words freezing, brittle breathed, in the air outside, they carried with them a gall storm, and who better to weather it than bent and drunken Monkey Abe. A misshapen and simple galoot, how could he have any feelings to hurt? But he did have feelings, in his feet and ankles, whose open sores had given him grief, septic and crippling, and left him hobbling for years.

When the doctors finally told him his feet would have to go, quipping he could bronze them like baby shoes, "Or, better yet," they said, "you could take them to Everett Sharpe to be stuffed and then sit them on your porch to greet visitors like Elspeth Campbell did with her companion goat, Chewie" (they snorted and laughed), he had to balk. Monkey Abe had borne many an aspersion on his back without complaint—they gave him purpose in those moments between drinks—but his feet, weakened and degenerated by disease, could not bear the attack, so he came to me and asked that I might say a few words to God on their behalf.

He sat on a table and swung his legs up. The stench and decay of those seeping and gnarled knots of flesh, unrecognizable as feet, recalled to me those days of sickness in Hong Kong, and I was steadied. I thought of my own broken ankle and how the bones had knit on the spot when Brother Durham sent the sanctified zap of healing snapping through my foot. I said, " 'Prepare ye the way of the Lord—make straight paths for His feet,' " John the Baptist's words rolling off my tongue easy as instinct, and I felt my hands float up and hang in the air over Abe's body, as though they were about to tug a marionette to life.

The feet like flippers, black and green, oozing, the original host disappeared behind sickness feeding on itself, the trembling of scared things, involuntary, nerves damaged, his face streaked with dirt and tears, hands crusted from years of disregard, kept strong enough to hold a cup, the plain green sickness of him, the trembling sickness, my hands shaking to meet such living death, the smell covering me like a film, an odor released to fend off predators, leave them wiping their eyes, the black and patches of yellow, toes lost in it, laid my hands right on the volcanic muck, deep into the dark swamp they went, felt the sticky atrophy, the erosion of will, fingers in the black, both of us trembling and I said, "God!" hands lost, roaming the range of disease, "Help this man!" Then the slight sway begun in my knees, the black so black it seemed silver, "Put your faith in Him. Aim it straight and believe," and the room rumbled, the table clanked, "Feel the Holy Spirit responding. It swirls about us, summoned by faith," until Abe rolled off the table and onto the floor, "Reach up and touch the hem of His garment!" body jumping, wired by the transfusion of Spirit, churning flesh on the floor, the clucking of Spirit words, sounds popped from his mouth, Abe spoke the language, words whose lack of meaning means everything, the utterance that opens the gates, the nothing burble of the divine, the language that's all inclusive, no one denied, words weightless as gossamer, unhindered by gravity, spoken and understood by all God's children, the tongues of angels filling their mouths, swallowing Jesus, the grace of knowing nothing, the all that nothing is, if only for a moment, and then the shaking stopped.

Abe had small scars, but the sickness was gone and he walked as he hadn't in years: he ran through the streets, a crier for Jesus.

When I think of those early days of the ministry, what I remember is the clear sense of purpose that possessed me and how struggle strengthened my will, left it lean as sinew. Those were the salad days of my resolve.

I traveled across America in my Packard, a shining, if mechanical, example of faith. The Gospel Car held together over land that was little more than wild terrain cleared of the impediments of boulders and trees, land little more than mud-slung ravines; its triumphs were due less to the ingenuity of Henry Ford than to the fact that it had places to go and people to honk at. There were souls waiting to be saved in the South.

Traveling through Georgia, Mississippi, Florida, I was struck not so much by the topographic and climatic contrast to my native Ontario as by the poverty, the unthinkable living conditions that seemed to stretch the length of the world. At night, beneath the moon, the earth curved against the light like a full belly, and I thought I could see the other side, but in the morning, things remained as before. The air was thick, as though you could spoon it out of your way; it was like breathing pudding.

My memory of that time is swollen with pictures, faded and yellow, of ramshackle lean-tos held together by prayer, scraps of soiled fabric that hung on matchstick bodies bent in all directions and hobbling without aim the way bodies that live against their will and better judgment sometimes do. This is what my remembering mind sees. Pictures of nothing, flat and barren blankness, the landscape gnawed to bone. And I remember the absence of animals.

I forged ahead and spread the word and though I lived a life to starve a Spartan, the kindness of townsfolk and the will of God kept my cup full to overflowing. Plainly stated, I was a success; the people flocked to my tent. I racked up soul after soul and spirits ran high, even in the midst of what seemed like so much lack in this country poised for war.

My sermons were a soothing salve to the sores hidden inside women. They amen-ed the loudest and theirs were always the first bodies to moan and roll with Spirit, so overcome were they with the abandon of divine union. I favored honey to vinegar, and they responded to the way I stressed grace above sin, their souls and nerves worn thin from trying to right that original wrong. They were also smitten with my revision of the principle of sanctification. I clutched at Christ's airy ankles and pulled him down to the ground. To be Christlike, I said, is to be human, mistaken and clumsy, not floating above, beyond pain and reproach. Perfection is fatal.

Women have always reached out to the wounds of Christ for alliance. It feels natural to us to live in a way that drives small holes through us, makes our brows, our feet and wrists bleed, scars our backs stooped from carrying guilt we never understood but took on faith. Women cheered and formed long lines when conversion seemed to them akin to clearing the slate.

Curiosity was piqued by the plain vexation of it all: A woman, preaching, on her own, in a car, in a tent, on the road? Such a strong voice and sturdy ankles. And that cape she wears. Who is she? Where's she from? What's her story?

And the colored folk. They packed the tent and blew it open with joyful screams and songs. They took to my God-gab easily,

126

let my words slip into their ears and through to their hearts, veins and arteries ballooning with love. Of course a ruckus was raised: To think, a little woman gallivanting across the country, waving the Bible as though she'd written it herself, a lady preacher, imagine! (She's no Billy Sunday, no siree bob.) And consorting with coloreds to boot! If that don't beat all. Traveling and speaking and singing among them, the dim light of her clearly at ease among the dark shadows. Always butting her head against boundaries, that one, as though they were just there to be stretched, rules nothing more than rubber to her. Jesus, Joseph, Mary, and Henry! Just who does this preacher woman think she is?

But the real scandal came in Key West, when neighboring flocks of white folks, God-starved, poured into colored town, stormed the tent and stood alongside their brown-skinned brethren. And there were those who said, *Surely the clompity-clomp of the four horsemen is audible in the distance when a white woman draws together a motley crowd of coloreds and whites, packed into the small space of a circus tent, exchanging breath and knocking knees, and saints preserve us, worshipping the same G-O-D!* And I said, *Forgive them, Father, for they are small and frightened, deprived of the benefit of bears.*

I know the story you wait for is the one where I fall, the one that exposes my Iscariot skin. But clinging to expectations can only end badly. Ask Jesus.

I lived my life by the signs. In 1916 the war in Europe raged like an inextinguishable fire, fed by fields of blood, a braid of bodies across the continent spelling out, with twisted limbs, a language I hoped my country would not have to speak.

We heard such terrible stories.

I have always preferred saving souls to bodies. Souls are simply more bankable, and with bodies you always run the risk of a poor performance, having to rely on props you can't control. But my reputation caused my tent to bulge with every infirmity imaginable, and the demands of the crowd kept my hands busy. Don't misunderstand—I have always had a place in my heart for the flesh. It is hard to get to nothing through the insistent corporeality of legs and necks and kidneys, but there is no other way. After all, the body is the site where faith becomes fact as the geyser of Holy Spirit gushes to the surface.

But I knew when my calcium-carbide lamp exploded in my face and the flames raced across my throat and shoulders, my cheeks and scalp, when I smelled the smell of my own hair burning down to nothing like fuses, I knew my sermons would soon have to shift from salvation to consolation, from Heaven to hope. When the fire was out, I laid my hands to my face and felt the blisters flatten; I felt the fevered skin cool. Then I saw how very small my hands seemed, the limited balm.

It wasn't long after the burning incident that the Germans sank the Lusitania, the same ship Robert and I had taken to visit his mother in Ireland before embarking for China. I remember his mother squeezing my arm and saying, "He's fragile. He's always been so fragile." The lines around her eyes were tight with fear. She could see across the ocean into the future. She leaned over and kissed my flat stomach.

The world was at war. Thousands of people died daily in ways heretofore unimagined. God watched and kept to Himself. I sang songs about mystery, redemption, and war bonds. I dreamt Kaiser Wilhelm crept into my tent one night and breathed poison gas into my sleeping face. He crawled away, into a trench, and said, "Jesus is the same today, yesterday, and forever: dead. The sun has set on deities."

Guided by the intuitive lurch of the Gospel Car, I followed my calling to the North.

Influenza is such a beautiful word. It sounds like a rare flower that blooms only at night.

128

The numbers of bodies that mounted from the epidemic began to exceed those of Americans killed in the war. In New York, as I tried to save souls, bodies were lost, two hundred a day the headlines read. There was a shortage of coffins and the dead lay rotting and unburied. That smell clung to the clothes and the hair of the living. It crawled into your nose and filled your mouth. I imagined I could taste the decay. I indulged my morbidity. I ran my tongue across my teeth and thought, *I've a bit of diseased lung caught between my molars,* or, *A bitter bowel rests beneath my tongue.* It made the ubiquitous flesh unreal. It was all I could do to keep from giving my own body up to the stacks of canceled lives.

When my threadbare dress gave up the ghost, I replaced it with a look befitting that of the ministering angel I hoped to be. I bought a stiff white uniform and together with the black cape that flapped behind me like wings when I walked, I conjured the image of a Savior-sent field nurse, and that's how I saw myself, a nurse tending the wounds of the sick souls at home.

The crowds continued to grow. So many flagging spirits in need of buttressing. I sensed a new approach was called for. People needed a respite from the woes of war and illness. They needed someone else's story, someone else's drama.

The Wise and the Foolish Virgins.

There are women, players, ten women carrying lamps, dressed in white, virgins, going to meet the Bridegroom, off to marry the King, the luckiest of women, they clutch their sleeves, expectant and fearful, at the door of King Jesus, the hearts beating quick in their chests like hummingbirds, sweet women, fed on dates and almonds, here to meet Him, the One, the Only, they laugh and pinch each other's cheeks, flushed and ready, their legs ache, they've saved themselves, no one has been allowed near enough to catch their scent, their feet stretch with yearning inside their shoes, their stomachs are hot, they feel a tug in their navels, they sway, they jump, the light flickers. They lie on the ground and sleep. In dreams they see Him. His teeth are crooked, but they don't mind. His lips are full, filled with color, body so thin, white marble, a lover's body, then see-through, beautiful ribs and heart floating behind the glass of his chest, they shift in their sleep, put their fingers in their mouths, to have and to hold, that curling white snake of spine, organs floating like fish in a tank, they tap-tap, cover their mouths and giggle, in sickness and in health, taut thighs, lawfully wedded, legs that have run far, from this day forward, hair coiling everywhere, feet and hands healed, ready to touch, to give and receive, and they wake, hungry, look for cakes and wine. They find their lamps filled with oil and burning, and here is where the cautionary split occurs. The wise ones, five of them, virgins and anxious, they dance and kiss each other's lips, practice for the real thing. The others, so foolish, untrusting, they question, this oil, where did it come from? What will it cost us? We haven't much, we're only virgins, we didn't ask for this oil, blood from a turnip, take it back, and then they claw their cheeks and tear their hair, they weep to see their sisters being carried to Heaven on the strong arms they all dreamt of.

The virgins bowed. The crowd was silent, breathing. Women looked at the men sitting near them. Men looked at their arms. I had them. They all closed their eyes and dreamt of salvation.

Is He coming? How is He coming? When and for whom is He coming? It was to this inquiry that I addressed my early life. And later: Who is He? What is He? How do I get them to see what I don't? And, finally, what's in a pronoun? One that towers like origin even among predicates, as if He were the only subject in the sea. Alpha and Omega indeed. As you may have guessed, the slip of my faith began to show.

The rest you know. It's a story you've heard, the one that gets told. I moved to Los Angeles, a place where my pomp and celebrity flourished. I became wealthy and gilded my sermons with fountains of water and wired angels that flew across stage, trained animals, a llama, a bear, hundreds of dancing feet, a spectacle. Sometimes I rode in on a motorbike or swung across stage on a rope, an evangelical Busby Berkeley, they said. At first I couldn't empty myself fast enough for the money that flowed in. Then there was debt, heavy as lead, the ballast I tried to evade.

And the too familiar story. Alcohol, adultery. Neglectful mother. I died then rose again (that's an old one). I disappeared into the ocean then resurfaced later, stooped with fatigue and a desperate tale of abduction. Despite my followers' unwavering belief in my integrity, my goodness, the authorities found my story pocked with implausibility. I was charged with corruption of morals and obstruction of justice. The beginning.

And there is more. And nothing.

In Angelus Temple, I stopped speaking the language of angels. I put pills on my tongue instead. I swallowed. This makes a good story.

The night before I was to deliver my sermon entitled "The Story of My Life," I groped in the dark for the bottle of barbiturates. You will say it was an accident. You will say I killed myself. You will say I went to meet my Bridegroom.

But this story must end.

This story, this life is not true. I told you. The truth is I died when I was ten years old, mauled by a bear. The truth is I died of a broken heart. The truth is I died giving birth. I died of malaria alone in a hospital in China. I died consumed in flames, an accident. I died beneath the feet of an angry crowd when a boy fell and crawled toward his crutches. The truth is I hung myself from a tree after surgery gave me no peace. But you know the truth is I'm lying and this admission is enough to make you believe.

I lived knowing I made myself up. You dreamt I was real. The story ends here where I am a hole you look into to see yourself.

Because I am nothing, I can make you believe.

Sherman and the Swan

Sherman likes mayflies, admires them for their courage, their quick impulse to propagate, in the face of their brief life span; they are sudden and fleeting things. Sherman dislikes firearms. He cannot understand how something clearly intended for wounding or killing can have its own national association and how the president of the United States can belong to such an organization.

Sherman's parents used to worry about Sherman's likes and dislikes, though they worried from a distance. They believed it unwise to get too close too fast. This is what they told Sherman. When he tried to hug them or squeeze their hands, they pushed him back by the shoulders, and Sherman's father would say, "Whoa, little man! What have I told you? You know what will happen if we spoil you rotten? People will say, 'Phew! What smells?' and they won't want to be near you." Sherman is fearful of smelling bad and driving people away, so he complies and tries not to touch. He imagines people he would like to be close to coughing from the fetid air around him, pushing him back, their arms growing and growing, stretching to such a distance they become stick figures and push him into a hush of icy water.

Sherman's mother had reservations about this method of child rearing. Sherman overheard her ask his father, "Are you sure we will be close-knit? Do you promise this will work? He's only a little boy." Sometimes at night Sherman could hear his mother weeping; the sound was soft, muffled, and made Sherman think of flannel, something he could rub up against, wrap himself in.

Sherman has lived with both of his parents for the twelve years he's been alive. They recently separated and both have begun to modify their parenting techniques. Sherman's mother touches his face now whenever she sees him. His father takes him places, hockey games, observatories, putting greens, hardware stores. They are often in a car together, buckled in, looking through glass, moving forward. Despite peer pressure, Sherman loves his parents.

Five years before Sherman was born, his sister, Melanie, was born. Melanie was tiny, always the smallest person in her class, and she was very pale beneath her occasional sallow tint. In the final picture of Melanie, a tiny arm barely larger than a feeding tube rests on the raised metal guard of her hospital bed. This arm is feathered with fine, white hairs and upstages the blurred face that fades into the pillow. When Sherman looks at this picture, he focuses on the arm. It looks to him like something in an early developmental stage, something that will eventually grow and bend and sprout and flourish into a beautiful, velvet white wing. Something that could lift a person up and out of any situation and deliver her to a body of water. Something that could save her from the threat of a predator or extinction. Sherman knows it is only a tiny, sick arm in the picture, but it seems obvious to him that we are all descended from a race of strong and elegant birds.

Sherman knows the story of his existence and wonders if other children know why they are here on earth, know if they've been brought for some true and special purpose or if they are only an accidental collision of elements, an extension of lineage, a repository for genes. Sherman was conceived as a means to a beginning, an instrument for prolonging life, and his parents have been quite forthcoming with the story behind his birth. There are even newspaper articles that document their intent. Melanie had leukemia and fell out of remission a year before Sherman was conceived. As the days passed and red spots bloomed on her legs and arms and her white hair thinned, family members were screened as possible candidates for the donation of bone marrow. But it is a specialized substance, and Melanie's parents soon realized that they would have to take the situation into their own hands, would have to create their own donor. Of course, there were no guarantees.

* * *

Sherman is in love with a fat girl named Cassie. There are two fat girls named Cassie at Horace Mann Elementary and one girl who claims to be big-boned named Cassandra, but it is Cassie Shockley with whom he is in love. Cassie's full name is Cassiopeia Prudence Shockley, and Sherman wishes to marry her one day and take her name because he loves the sound of Sherman Shockley. It is not quite as good as if her last name were Tank, but he has looked in the phone book to find that people with this name do not exist.

Sherman and Cassie sit at opposite ends of a seesaw. Sherman is slight and his end of the seesaw is elevated several feet off the ground. This is one of the reasons he likes Cassie. He likes to dangle his feet and imagine he is on a giant tongue depressor, a Lilliputian; or he pretends he is seated in an ancient and impossibly slow catapult. Sherman loves being up in the air. He feels indefinite and brave.

A clump of children near the merry-go-round disperses, radiating in different directions like a slow burst of fireworks. As Jason Piper passes the seesaw, he says, "Later, 'gators."

"Alligators can adjust their body temperatures in order to determine the sex of their offspring," says Cassie.

This is another reason Sherman loves Cassie. She knows many strange and wondrous things, though Sherman recognizes her knowledge is occasionally dubious. She once told him she knew for a fact that kissing could not, in and of itself, cause pregnancy, but kissing before the age of thirteen could cause a girl's breasts to overdevelop. She could not decide whether this was an altogether undesirable effect.

"How do they know which sex to want?" asks Sherman.

"I think it all depends on their disposition. If they are prone to fatigue, naturally they want girl alligators because girl alligators are smart and quiet and contentedly sit in the cool mud. But if the mothers thirst for adventure and don't mind constant roughhousing, then they want boys. Boy alligators stick their scaly noses into everything and eat smelly things that aren't good for them." Cassie rests her elbows on puffy, pink knees.

"Well, what if one day all the alligator mothers had a tired disposition and had only girls, then alligators would be out of business. Anyway, it sounds prejudiced, Cas." Sherman kicks his feet as he speaks.

136

"I can't help my female perspective." Cassie starts to untie her tennis shoes. "I've got blisters all over my feet from skating Saturday. Let's pop them."

Sherman swings one leg over and dismounts the seesaw. He is afraid to touch Cassie's feet. He is afraid he won't be able to control himself. He wants more than anything to wrap his arms around her waist as far as they'll go and to quickly kiss the soft putty of her cheek. He wants to bury his face in her bulging stomach. He loves that there is excess Cassie. He wants to be romantic and witty and tell her the rings of flesh around her heavenly body are lovely; she is his little Saturn. But he knows she is self-conscious and dreams of a different body, and he fears if they get too close, she will discover his soul has a terrible odor and she will be repelled.

"I've got to feed Aretha."

Cassie stares at her feet. "They look like they've been bubble-wrapped. Who'd have thought skating could do so much damage? I might have to go to a foot guy." Cassie pushes tentatively against a blister as if it were a dead bug.

"Podiatrist."

"What I said."

"You just need to skate more often. Build up calluses."

"And have alligator feet? No way, José."

"Way," Sherman says and smiles.

Cassie puts her socks back on. "Can I come see Aretha? My mom's at the beauty shop until 4:30."

"I don't know. This is our quiet time together. I think it'd hurt her feelings if I brought my girlfriend home at this time of day, though she probably wouldn't let it show." Sherman runs his hands through the brown tufts of his hair. Sherman's hair is coarse and prefers standing up to lying down, which it will not do without a struggle. Yesterday Cassie cut and styled it in such a way that it looks as if it grows in clusters like sage or endive. Sherman is happy it now obeys without the use of styling gel.

"Looks good," Cassie says, smiling and nodding.

"Aretha's probably screaming for her duckweed. I'll see you tomorrow, Cas." Sherman smiles and walks backward for as long as the terrain feels safe and familiar.

*   *   *

Aretha is a trumpeter swan. It was a little over a year ago when Sherman decided to play outside so that his parents would not have to whisper their grievances to one another, and he walked to the lake, where he spotted a huge nest on the margin. Swans had nested there before, and he knew not to disturb them, but this mother swan was slumped over and quiet. As Sherman neared the nest, he realized the swan was too silent and supine to be alive. He petted the long, white neck and felt under her wings. Her body was still warm. He covered her with his jeans jacket and built a small fire, then he ran all the way to Lodema's, the bird lady's, house.

Lodema's trees were feathery, flaming with chickens and magpies. Sherman could see the owls and pigeons and ducks and hawks recuperating in their respective pens. Sherman loved to visit Lodema. The inside of her house was filled with beautiful domesticated birds that played on rubber rings dangling from the branches of a huge oak tree. The tree reached through the center of her living room toward the skylight of her roof. Some of the birds would swoop to Sherman's shoulder when he went near the tree. Others would say "hello" when the phone rang or "come in" when there was a knock on the door. Colonel Klink, an African Grey, cracked nuts and fed them to Lodema. Sherman loved how the birds took care of her. He knew people thought Lodema was eccentric, but he decided this was a good thing. His parents were wary of this association initially but eventually deemed it beneficial. Lodema told Sherman she had been born under the zodiacal sign of Aquarius and Aquarians were always eccentric. And since he was a Gemini with, she discovered, a rising sign of Aquarius, she assured him they would always get along famously.

When Lodema got to the nest, the swan was beginning to cool. Lodema kissed its black bill and bowed before it. She cried. She wrapped the clutch of four eggs in a plush towel and placed this on a hot water bottle in a cardboard box. Together she and Sherman quickly buried the mother swan in the moist earth near the lake.

"What happened to her?" Sherman asked.

"Probably ate some old lead. The hunters get them one way or another, sometimes years after they aim for them. Used to use them for pillows and powder puffs."

After several weeks, Lodema gave Sherman the last egg as it appeared to be infertile. Sherman asked to borrow an incubator just in case and within two days Aretha was born. Sherman watched all day as she poked bits of shell out of her way and unfolded her crumpled body into the open air.

With an eyedropper he fed her a mixture of instant baby food and a powdered concoction Lodema fed to her larger birds. He swirled the white fuzz on Aretha's head as he fed her.

When she opened her eyes, Sherman stared into the small black bubbles. He thought he saw himself, saw how his lips curved and jutted as if for some specialized purpose. He saw how his tiny ears were invisible beneath his unruly hair. He felt aerodynamic. He breathed deeply. He wanted to know what it felt like to glide through the air that passed through him and fueled his own movement. Aretha gurgled and yapped in scratchy tones. She inched toward him, and he kissed her black bill. She nuzzled his moist palm. She tried to pass through it, to disappear in the callused flesh. Sherman felt newly born, engendered by a baby swan, a sweet and needy cygnet.

When Sherman's parents found out he had hatched a swan and was hiding it, caring for it in his room, they were not angry. They thought it would be good and educational for him to have such an exotic pet; they thought it would teach Sherman responsibility, so they fixed a place for it in Sherman's father's work shed. They did not know it was an endangered species. They did not know the swan's lineage was in jeopardy, that the mother swan had been struggling unconsciously against the extinction of her race, that the baby swan's birth was purposeful.

Sherman knew and Lodema knew. Lodema said there wasn't anything to do now that Aretha had been imprinted. Sherman knew what this meant. He knew his image had been branded on the black beads of her eyes, and he knew her need for him had been etched in a deeper place, a place beneath the gray and white down, a place where sentience and instinct and emptiness collide. And he, too, felt this in the pit of himself.

Lodema told Sherman to tell people that Aretha was a basic garden variety swan and hope she wouldn't start her migrant bugling in front of anyone who might care. "They're not as endangered as they used to be. There are several thousand of them now. They got down to a couple hundred at the time old Audubon was painting pictures of them with their own quills," Lodema said.

*   *   *

When Sherman gets home, Aretha is chasing squirrels in the front yard. Sherman's house sits far back from the street. His parents own the several acres of wooded land surrounding it. The house itself is sequestered by a huddle of pin oaks filled with squirrels and birds. Aretha never ventures farther than a few hundred feet away from the house without Sherman.

Sherman wonders what Aretha thinks she is. A dog or a small boy perhaps. He knows she has no concept of swan. She seems unimpressed by all types of birds. She frequently quarrels with the persnickety blue jays and charges robins as they tug something from the earth.

When Aretha spots Sherman coming down the path, she lurches toward him on the black spatulas of her feet; the seven foot-wings spread dramatically, as if beckoning his embrace. Sherman cannot help but see the soap-opera quality of this ritual: they are long-parted lovers with names like Lance and Ashley and tragic pasts coming together out of nowhere in a field undulating with wildflowers or wheat. It reminds him of a commercial for a feminine hygiene spray, a commercial he once saw while watching television with Cassie and which made him turn a near Day-Glo pink. And yet he felt comforted to know women must also worry about love and odor.

Sherman falls on the ground and Aretha leaps on top of him, squawking and nibbling his cheeks and throat. He sits up and buries his face in her breast and kisses the squirming white pillow. "I have a surprise for you," he says. He leads her to the shed. She waddles alongside, nipping at the fingers that will feed her.

In the shed, she sits quietly on her blanket, the hooked neck poised and still. Sherman digs in his backpack. "I stopped at the lake and got you some water buttercups and elodea," he says.

As Sherman feeds her, he strokes the conveyer belt of bumps along her throat. He feels the invisible hump in her sternum housing the large windpipe that allows her to trumpet. "Cassie told me something about you today. She said that ancient Germanic peoples believed swans embodied the souls of dead people. They thought swans were sacred and holy." Sherman remembers Aretha's mother, her long neck lolling over the side of the nest. "I wonder where the souls of swans go," he says.

*   *   *

Sherman turns over to see the red numbers on his clock read 4:17. He expels a "hey" when he notices a figure seated at the end of his bed. He sits up and turns on the table lamp. It is his grandfather, his father's father, Elmer, a dead person. They stare at one another for several minutes. Sherman was six years old when they last saw each other.

Sherman says, "Grandpa Elmer?"

Elmer smiles.

Sherman bites into his lower lip to see if he can feel pain. He can. He reaches out and touches Elmer's hand. He can feel the knotted, leathery skin. "You're solid," he says.

"Yes."

"Are you still dead?"

"Yes."

"What are you doing here?" Sherman wonders if he is psychic, if his mind and body somehow conduct the currents of spirits. He feels light as a Kleenex.

Elmer maneuvers his false teeth and holds them between his lips. Sherman laughs at this old trick. Elmer returns the teeth to his mouth. Sherman becomes serious and silent, then asks, "Have you seen Melanie?"

Elmer nods.

"Is she okay? Are her arms bigger? Is she strong?" The fact that his grandpa still wears false teeth worries Sherman. He would have thought everything would be repaired in the afterlife.

Elmer says, "She is good. She is happy."

"Is she still sick?"

Elmer shakes his head. "She has big pink wings and webbed feet so she can land on the water."

"Do you know God?" Sherman asks.

Elmer shrugs his shoulders. "As well as anyone, I suppose."

"Have you seen Elvis?"

"Too many impersonators to be sure." Elmer smiles and squeezes Sherman's feet through the blanket.

142

"Is the Virgin Mary really a virgin?" Sherman smiles.

"She's given me no reason to doubt her," Elmer says. He pulls a cellophane-wrapped cigar out of his shirt pocket. He holds it out to Sherman. "They don't make these anymore," he says. He puts the cigar back in his pocket.

Sherman asks, "Why do things become extinct?"

Elmer stands. "I don't know," he says. "Just because I'm dead doesn't mean I have all the answers."

✳   ✳   ✳

Cassie and Sherman are sitting in his front room, watching television. With remote control in hand, Sherman flips from channel to channel to channel.

"You have an abnormally short attention span," Cassie says.

"There's nothing good on anyway."

"Why can't we play with Aretha?"

"I told you, she's jealous. She'd just charge you like she did yesterday."

"She needs to get used to me." Cassie reaches into the pocket of her jeans jacket.

Sherman does not want Aretha to get used to Cassie. He does not want them to bond. He knows they could give one another something he doesn't have, some secret strength. He knows they would crouch together under trees, laughing and honking, and they'd hush when they saw him approaching. Then his love for them would sour. It would begin to reek of the thing he could not give them, the thing that could lift them up and save them.

Cassie pulls crayons out of her pocket: maize, raw umber, periwinkle blue. She says, "They've replaced these colors. I think we should start a time capsule and keep track of all the things that have been discontinued, things indicative of the sorry time we live in."

Sherman flips past more programs, a fleeting collage of moving pictures. He doesn't want to think about things that have been discontinued. He settles on a program about killer bees.

Cassie says, "The leaf-cutting ants of Central America are farmers, and they grow their own food. They gather leaves and grow a special kind of fungus that they live off of. And they know how to weed the undesirable fungi out. They're quite resourceful and self-reliant. They don't need crumbs or honey or human flesh to survive." Cassie leans over and kisses Sherman on the cheek. "My mom put me on another diet," she says. "It's all rice cakes and broccoli. And carrots, carrots, carrots. It's barely enough to sustain a small breed of rabbit." Cassie stares at the layers of her stomach. "We have to be careful of my ketones this time."

Something wells up inside Sherman and he lurches toward Cassie and knocks her back to the floor. He kisses her nose then buries his lips in the soft center of each new breast. He jumps up and runs out the door.

He runs and runs through the woods, past the lake, across the barren highway, until he comes to the Fairgrove Shopping Center. He runs toward Safeway and collapses in the first parking space on the blue wheelchair symbol. He lies on his back and looks up at the letters that spell out SAFEWAY. There is a nest of finches cupped in the bottom curve of the S. The tiny birds flit about, squeeze through letters, and perch on the F and the E. Sunlight slants across WAY. The birds on top of the sign face the light, as if they were phototropic, as if they were drawn toward the wavy heat by something deep inside their thin, translucent bones. Sherman watches the nervous and luminous activity of the birds until an old man yells out of his car, "Hey, kid! You better get up unless you want to be squashed like a bug." Some boys walk by and laugh and say, "Road pizza."

Sherman whispers, "Dead meat."

144

* * *

Today is Saturday, the day and night Sherman spends with his father. Before Sherman left, his mother hugged him hard, pressing the breath right out of him, and he felt as if he'd been knocked on his back. She kissed him on the mouth and her lips were wet and sweet. She clutched his face in her hands and said, "I love you, Sherman. I always have, and you're all that matters to me now." She let go of his cheeks, and her eyes, clear and empty as water, stared past him at his father's car in the driveway. She laughed, and her lips quivered. "You're the only reason it's not obscene for me to still be alive."

As Sherman got into his father's car, he watched his mother standing in the doorway. She held one hand over her mouth and clutched her skirt with the other. Her face was tense and furrowed, as if she were crying, although she wasn't, as though she were watching her only child go off to war and imagined him coming back with fewer limbs or relentless dreams of dying. Sherman has seen this look before, in old photographs.

* * *

Sherman and his father sit in the green-shag-carpeted living room of his father's apartment. Sherman's father drinks a beer he has heavily salted, and with the TV remote he flips from golf to tennis. "So, what should we do, Sport?" Sherman's father smiles and raises his eyebrows. He drops the remote and rubs his stomach.

Sherman blinks consciously and listens for the rumble he feels in his intestines. He thinks it is interesting how a person can feel his stomach growl before he can hear it, sort of like thunder and lightning. He doesn't like to be called Sport, though he prefers it to Little Man or Sherm.

"So? What do you say? We could go hunting. Mum's the word to your mother, of course. I just got some new boots, and we could borrow my neighbor's rifle. I don't know dick about hunting,

145

but we could teach each other. Don't want you turning into no mama's boy, do we?" Sherman's father laughs and attempts to ruffle Sherman's stiff hair.

"No," says Sherman. "That would be tragic."

His father tightens his lips. "Well, let's hear your bright ideas, Einstein. I don't know how to entertain a twelve-year-old kid. I feel like we're on some goddamned blind date or something."

Sherman wishes he were cryogenically frozen inside a time capsule, lying next to a twisting hologram of Elvis and a stack of electric toothbrushes, waiting to be thawed by a distant culture. "I heard they were doing military maneuvers in the forest on the opening day of hunting season," Sherman says. He stares at his clasped hands.

"No shit? Anybody get hurt?"

"A lot of animals."

*　　*　　*

Sherman's father sleeps on the couch as people on television jump from bridges and dangle by bungee cords like rubber spiders. The afternoon sun angles through the sliding glass doors and spotlights his white belly. Sherman stares at the dust motes that tumble through the light and quietly sings, "We are here, we are here, we are here. Boil that dust speck, boil that dust speck, boil that dust speck." He turns the television off and walks to his father's bedroom. He runs his hand over the items on his father's dresser: a curved wallet molded by his father's hip, a pair of cuff links, a golf tee, a Tiparillo cigar box, and cologne in green and brown bottles shaped like an old car and a horseshoe. Sherman opens the cigar box. It is full of old photographs. He looks at a picture of his father in the army. His father is thin and stiff and his hair is cut short and neat as a newly mown lawn. The scowl on his face seems rehearsed. There is a vertical series of black-and-white pictures of his parents.

They laugh, they kiss, they hug, they smile. Sherman thinks they look like actors demonstrating the different nuances of "happy" for a screen test. The rest of the pictures are all of Melanie. They are in chronological order from her birth picture, in which she is wrinkled and brown like an old vegetable, to a picture of her in a swimming pool. Melanie stands thin and white in the middle of the shallow end of the pool. Her face bears no expression; her eyes are closed. She holds out a hand, and it is unclear whether she is waving or asking someone to stop.

*   *   *

Sherman takes Aretha to the lake for a swim. He fed her beforehand so she would not be tempted to dig in the dangerous depths where the poisonous substances lurk. He knows it is risky to swim after eating, but he feels bringing a hungry swan to the site of her mother's last supper would be a bigger gamble. Besides, he is not sure it is possible for a swan to have a cramp. Sherman suspects the idea of deadly cramps resulting from swimming too soon after eating, which he has never experienced or witnessed himself, is a myth manufactured by adults who secretly hope that the lulling effects of turkey sandwiches and milk or the heaviness of meatloaf will sink their children to sleep, and make them forget entirely about swimming.

Aretha immediately paddles out into the center of the lake. She snaps at water striders and dips her head underwater. Sherman loves the shape of her head and neck: a question mark, a pitcher handle, half a heart. Sherman's own neck feels hot, inflamed. His face stings. He is thinking of a million things at once. Wishes and desires and regrets bleed together behind his eyes. There is Cassie, healthy and pink-skinned. Her mother says she is full-figured. She is ringed with flesh, and Sherman felt the feathery give of her breasts as he pressed his lips to them. There's his mother, who drinks can after can of Coke in the dark and hugs him now when she thinks he's asleep and talks to him in an altered voice, as if he were a cat or a doll. Then there's Aretha and her fragile species. He remembers the moment she first opened her eyes and he saw himself etched in the black circles; she pushed herself into the nest of his hands. Now his hands can barely cradle her head, and he fears they will only grow smaller as she ages, but he will feed her and he will love her and she will live many swan years.

Aretha flaps and honks and swims in circles. Sherman wishes he, too, had huge wings and thinks he can almost feel pinfeathers poke through the skin on his back. He wishes he were younger so he could pretend, pretend he was a swan and Aretha his mate.

Sherman begins to undress. He removes his sneakers and socks, his jacket and T-shirt and jeans and underwear. He walks into the water. The water is so cold it feels to him as if his flesh and bones were leaving him, melting, decomposing with each step, as if he were becoming part of the water.

They would live in an enormous nest atop the woven sticks of a beaver house. They would eat insects and tubers, snails and small fish. They would have beautiful children, small, fuzzy cygnets, remarkable for their blue eyes.

Aretha sees him enter the water and begins to swim toward him. His knees and elbows and ankles ache, and he wonders if Aretha can feel him course through her thin, hollow bones. Sherman extends his arms and closes his eyes. He is not sure if he is beckoning or warning.

Secession, XX

On the thirteenth day following fertilization, "we" found "ourselves" with three X's and a Y to work with, so it didn't take brain surgeons, or even budding geneticists, for the excessive zygote we were to figure out how best to assemble ourselves. We were the thwarted hermaphrodite splitting defiantly down the middle, reconciled to sharing intestines, a bit of pelvis, perhaps a spleen, but not everything. We knew enough each to claim an X, and then I said *Girl* and yanked the other X out of the communal

The biological impossibility of our zygosity proved no deterrent to my sister.

XXOO, she signed our postcards from summer camp (where we were the envy of all sack racers). This valediction was not meant to signify affectionate gestures, vouchers for kisses and hugs that could be cashed in upon our return (she occasionally drew half arrows shooting northeast out of the O's to make this unmistakably clear). It was she on the left and I on the right. To her, I was absence from the stewpot. He (to be) looked on and blinked, so in burgeoning disgust I finally punted the crippled X, amputee, that hobbling, one-legged Y, over to It, deciding his Himness. I could see that He né It, future brow in a phantom crimp, would have pondered ontological mind-benders all day had I not taken decisive action. Where would we be now had I been as equivo-cal as we seemed fated to be? Perhaps swapping sex like shoes—today the yob, testicles descending, Flor-sheims polished and reflect-ing redundant chins as we bent to tie them; tomorrow a filly, donning a frock, legs crossed tightly as the clasp of a coin purse, retracting the truncheon, passing it un-der the table like a secret, internal relay, Mary Janes kicking the curious dog as he wags by sniff-sniffing. You can imagine what fa-tiguing work it would be to cobble together an identity out of such fleshy ambiva-lence. So I drew a line in

start. The space harnessed, circumscribed by Her.

She told me once she'd dreamt boys were small as beetles, and she caught them and put them in killing jars, prodding them with a pen-cil when they got too lippy, feeding them blades of grass through the holes in the lid when they pleaded for rations.

We performed theater in the summer, on a stage of rick-ety orange crates covered in burlap. She wrote soliloquies for me that invariably ended: HIM: *(spoken plaintively)* Y, y me?

She made my circulation quicken, her desperation for *sovereign contours.*

the genetic sand and it has divided us (zippered together though we are like conjoined sleeping bags) ever since.

Some nights I stroke his face as he sleeps, feel a tingle in my own. I will him not to stir and he doesn't. He heeds the messages I send him through the beats of our hearts, palpitations we've learned to compose and decipher like Morse code—thum-thump thumpity-thump: Don't Move. And I know he does the same to me, caresses me in sleep as intimately as congenital disease. A residue of sensation sometimes pinks my throat as I wake in the morning.

Naturally, we do everything together. Even if we weren't soldered along the torso, I don't think he would ever have left my side (though he dreamed of little else). When we were children, our parents always told us they were doubly blessed, as they grinned at us tragically. *And so are you,* they'd insist, having as we did the peculiar honor of sharing

Her cool fingers against my cheek made me well up uncomfortably with tender feeling, and I'd begin to gulp air. It was as though I'd been knocked on my back and was struggling to recover lost breath. I did not think of her in these moments. It was my mouth I imagined kissing.

I never ache to leave her, though I do occasionally dream of receiving postcards sent from places with brightly plumed tropical birds or slick-haired dictators on the stamps. XX, she signs them simply so I know it's her.

skin and bone, internal organs bridging that gulf of Otherness that renders the rest of humanity small and cheerless, discrete, forsaken (honor schmonor, anima and animus warring under one tent, launching missiles in a relentless covert land grab, thought I petulantly in those moments when I yearned for autonomy. "Beat it!" I'd sometimes bleat aloud instead of think, and my brother just clasped his hands and endured, the saucer-eyed supplicant). "That's what we all really hanker for," my mother once whispered to me, and she did frequently look upon us with eyes moist at the corners and narrowed with envy.

Most days, we took our blessing seriously. At my brother's urging, we practiced saintly behavior, gave nickels to the humpbacked, dirt-scabbed, addicted, and street-diseased people along the Paseo, people who slept in rusting, wobbly-wheeled shopping carts and donned a full wardrobe even in August,

I could sometimes feel her willfully hogging our organs, like a fitful sleeper tugging the blanket to her side of the bed. I felt her trying to digest me, me, little more than tough protein to her. She always stopped with only the faintest morsel of me remaining, and, somehow, against both our wills, I rallied, persisted. I think she feared how she might be transformed if I became more fuel than aimless appendage. I imagined myself impertinent blood washing through her veins, moving her arms and mouth and feet in discord with the neurotransmission of her wishes. I was never as harmless as she convinced herself I was. It wasn't subversion. I was reserved long before I understood it to be an asset, fundamentally laconic.

people with palm-sized army knives, packages of crumbled crackers, slim, green New Testaments, Tiparillos, and quarters cadged from blood-bank volunteers in their pockets. The people other people took circuitous routes to avoid pressed themselves against walls as we passed. We parted crowds, crowds of those who usually made others hasten their step. We were a freak's freak.

One day, on a visit to our maternal grandparents in Michigan, walking along the shore of Asylum Lake, my brother became fascinated with the Jesus bugs, those splay-legged insects that skate across water, sleek as geometry and weightlessly optimized to take advantage of surface tension. He was certain we were somehow equipped to do the same, on our archless feet, large for our size, flat as platypuses, so we stepped off the dock and onto the water, and for a second we hovered there, the water heavy as ballast that kept us, grown sheer

I had originally been one of two boys. We were Romulus and Remus floating down the Tiber of the fallopian tube in search of the appropriate site for the founding of an empire. My sister turned out to be the she-wolf waiting at the other end. When we came tumbling into her encampment, she pressed against her amnion and saw our chorion give, hold the shape of her hand. She gnawed an opening in her sac and then began working on ours, until she parted the curtains of membrane and stepped inside. As we would soon be bulging at the placental seams, she snipped the line at my brother's umbilicus and hooked me up to the potent generator of herself. Her hunger was not easily sated, though, and there were times when I saw her eyeing the cord, which coiled near my crown. I knew she was imagining it noosed round my neck

with divinity, from floating up into the sun, kept the thinning wax of being from melting off our bones. But I couldn't sustain the insubstantiality and I dropped into the drink, pulling my brother with me.

My brother has all the Jesus on his side. It was always me who ran after the kids who hurled chestnuts and hedge apples at us (in place of clever invectives, the snot-nosed galoots) as I schlepped my pacifist brother beside me like a lame appendage, so forgiving, civil, so disobedient to the genes flanking him scrappily to his right.

Sometimes we lie in the hammock, sunk deep in its belly, an inverse pregnancy. I move my mouth to his, kiss him, and it becomes confusing, whose lips are whose, whose chapped, whose sticky, whose molar is aching at that moment, but then I taste the bitter balm of godthefather on his lips, and I remember which mouth is mine and pull it back. When we take com-

and was willing the womb's trapdoor to drop so she'd be rid of me for good and could suck the choicest drops of marrow from that rope of life.

I strove to be pure, transparent as water, but I was vaguely aware that the very struggle to remain innocent made me regretfully wise. If there is anything I wanted never to be it is knowing. At our baptism, after the reverend sprinkled water on our foreheads with the dainty covertness of a person on a sodium-restricted diet salting an egg, I awoke to find the organist pressing athletically against my chest and water dribbling down my chin. I turned to see my sister glaring at me. I recalled looking up through gentle waves, without ambition, toward the water's surface.

munion on Christmas and
Easter, my brother (our soul's
emissary) laps the grape juice,
tries discreetly to dislodge the
host from his tooth with his
tongue, and, try as I might,
I can never stifle the belch
that rises up within me from
that hub of sutured selves,
that centrifugal nucleus that
seems to blow us out and
blow us out from the inside
and haunts us both with a
feeling of excess. I can see the
vapor of Jesus slip out of my
mouth like soap bubbles, pop
pop . . . pop, see him float
toward the pastor's clasped
hands. The pastor gazes past
us with an aspect of forbear-
ance that seems pasted to his
face with thin glue, a look
that appears as though it will
curl forward at any moment
like improperly hung wall-
paper and will reveal the hole
in the wall, the bottomless
despair beneath faith that
makes his soul gape. An un-
dressable wound—that's how
I've always thought of faith.

The rich repast of body
and blood are best taken with

food or milk lest you risk an ulceration of the spirit.

When we turned thirteen, my brother became suddenly modest. Though he showed a predilection for this at an early age, fig-leafing himself with his hands, averting his eyes from the exposed charm of his other half, he quickly recognized the impracticality of such behavior and distracted himself by looking through our body like a Viewmaster to gaze upon the silvery soul, unhampered by a bodily hedging of bets; he was buoyed by how it swam free of genitalia, floated inside us cleanly and purely with never the need to unzipper its trousers. Finally acquiescing to physical imperatives, he slumped on the toilet and occupied himself with chaste and hygienic thoughts, while I, happy to reclaim scatology from the stifling ether in which eschatology hung (it was lost on neither of us that the subtraction of the bodily from the heavenly left only a flip-flopped and befuddled

Honestly, it wasn't the body—even our body—that anguished me so much as the fluids it produced. They were so unpredictable and abundant, new eruptions daily. I longed to be arid as desert, desiccated. At night, in an attempt to subdue all geysers burbling within, I imagined thirstless pack animals and sand-blown sultans bent against hot siroccos. My sister, on the other hand, was perfectly at ease frolicking in any effluvium.

"he"), always marveled at the insider information I collected at such moments.

I have always loved my body, loved running my hands across hill and dale, loved the discovery of soft puckerings of flesh hidden in uncharted fissures. At night, as my brother withdrew, my hands roamed the merged continents of our body, noting the shifting topography of Pangaea's hemispheres, parched steppe to fertile grasslands. Though my brother's half seemed to respond pleasurably, seemed to enjoy being mapped, in the morning he would be quieter hunched over his oatmeal, seem more pale, nearly translucent, the white of a cooked turnip.

At school, junior high, the administration was stumped as to which compulsory class to place us in: home ec or shop. The answer seemed to be found in our dexterity, whether sewing machine or band saw posed less of a threat to our fingers, to our overlapped physiognomy. (I

My body is the very shape of betrayal. It rises and stiffens and purrs against all my considered remonstrations, wicked. My sister, my puppeteer. I have always been thin, thinner than my sister, hoarder of flesh, and so any new cleft or ripple is immediately visible, and my sister fingers the putty of me at night, tries to conjure her own likeness out of my spare clay.

knew well the picture class-mates' minds conjured as their thoughts moved from the spinning jagged teeth of the saw to my brother and me, though our grain went arm to arm, not head to toe, so they'd never be able to sever us neatly. *Better stick to spice racks*, I radioed back to them with my glare.) Actually, we were quite graceful, having had to thoughtfully choreo-graph every move. Harmony of gesture was a matter of bald well-being; injury lurked in every step, every impulsive swipe of the hand. If we were all joined at the hip, there'd be no war.

Standing in the principal's office, surrounded by admin-istrators, secretaries, PTA of-ficers, the school nurse, my brother became angry and pushed me. This was the first sign of antipathy toward me my brother had ever shown, and it thrilled me. Before this show of aggression, I think we both feared he was only an appended afterthought of yin to my anchoring yang, a per-

The economy of my disposi-tion was partly owing to the understanding that when I did speak, it was with my sis-ter's voice, the propulsion of her breath. She was curator of the lungs, you see. This became clear to me in junior high when we stood before the principal, waiting for him to administrate some decision with regard to our curricu-lum, which was gender spe-

functory gentility that merely lent a rough-hewn dignity to my intemperance. When my brother took the slingshot and pebble from my pocket and aimed it at me, our hearts clapped loudly inside us, and I understood—in this similarity of impulse—we were mete of discrete spirits, hinged, hyphenated, but fully forged.

You can imagine how the heart sank when he shot his own foot.

He was good to the root! In this moment I began to understand my own insufficiency, my lopsided wickedness, and I growled, causing Mr. Pelofsky, the principal, to drop his monogrammed fountain pen. Before, I had always quite enjoyed being a discipline problem, enjoyed hearing my brother yelp as the paddle met my backside; I held my ankles and grinned defiantly as the disciplinarian scratched his chin and pondered the shiftiness of justice, the social contract, considered, vaguely, sacrifice, the cific and involved machinery that made them fear litigation should we injure ourselves, which seemed to those dreamless bureaucrats likely. Watching my sister sneer at the principal's shriveled fig-faced secretary (what she was thinking as she looked at her), I suddenly realized that anything I might interject in the matter would be so thoroughly in relation to the wishes of my sister as to be moot where my own interests were concerned, and it further occurred to me that, when you got right down to it, I had no interests; if I ever had, they had long ago been so skillfully colonized as to have virtually disappeared from both mind and memory. This realization left me momentarily fractious, until I understood, in all the erosion of self—the horror and relief such recognition brings—that, like a boomerang, no matter where I aimed my loathing, it somehow always bent its trajectory and dropped at my own feet.

greater good, imagined how we—that is, my brother and I—might one day complicate not only corporal but capital punishment, saw one of us hanging from a noose, the other flailing about and gasping, begging for clemency not for himself but humankind, and pleading for acknowledgment of our interdependency, the executioner himself beginning to feel the prickle and burn of taut hemp against his throat, vertebrae cracking beneath the hood.

It was decided that too many liability quandaries were posed by our working with any sort of machinery and so Mrs. Ridgeway would instruct us in deportment during seventh period. Deported is just what we, aliens accidentally washed ashore the cloying nation of the other, each secretly longed to be.

A throng of memories always throbbed inside my brother and me as isolated moments trying to assemble themselves into a parliament

Were they my feet? I could no longer distinguish.

that could agree on a shared history, but, frequently bellicose, or at the very least churlish, competing versions of significant events often tried to muscle one another out, filibustering until the others slumped beneath their powdered wigs and gave in, wearied into submission. I could see as far back as synkaryon, which my brother and I still remain, a fusing never meant to be/never meant to be sundered. *Sin carrion*, I sometimes thought, the decaying roadside remains of our parents' original sin, the sin of ill-fated genes recklessly colliding. And *sin carry-on*, fateful luggage that went with us everywhere.

The blood my body let, internal leech of menses sucking the poison of fertility out, was the final betrayal, and my brother refused to eat or sing at choir (though his voice, unlike my own, had yet to drop, and so remained dulcet during hymns) or sleep much after that. He was affronted by this exclusion, the fumbling

It's true that I wasn't at all prepared for menstruation, despite that "You're Becoming a Woman" lecture at school I was made to sit in on. The sheer gooeyness of it was certainly objectionable, not to mention the backache and light-headedness I'd not anticipated, but what was most distressing was really

161

mess it created, the desecration of clean sheets, despite the fact that it was he who had traced his fingers along an imaginary perforation at night, wishing we might be severed like stamps, like soon-to-be distinct continents giving grudgingly, eagerly, in to the whims of plate tectonics. I felt the tug in the other direction when he dreamt of lying languorously on his side, leaning with disaffected panache against a wall, when he dreamt of swimming sidestroke, imagined walking with a blank peripheral prairie spreading out to either side. He squeezed his eyes closed and forced his thoughts to stack themselves vertically, pretended lateral dominion, tried to imagine what it would be like to be utterly alone. I had been stung by the vigor of his jerking when he was in the throes of such traitorous fantasies, but I yanked him back toward my side and held his nose until his mouth popped open like a split fruit and his eyes quit their seismographic

the questions it raised for me regarding transubstantiation. Uncannily, the onset of the bleeding coincided with Easter communion. The heresy of this! It was clear my sister bled to prove a point. Ingesting His resurrected flesh and blood had more abiding significance for her, the grape juice transformed, flowing undeniably from her loins. My sister claimed, with more one-upped smugness than conviction, that women bled to remind us of the wounds suffered for the piggishness of mankind. I concealed my revulsion lest she oink at me.

twitching beneath the lids. He always looked regretful in the morning, knowing even the shadowy terrain of his unconscious mind was hardly too formidable a frontier for a pioneer such as myself. What he desired most was secrecy, the thing he could never have stapled to a spy like me.

In eleventh grade, it came as a genuine revelation to us both (our premier epiphany—which was itself a revelation—the first uncovering of something concealed from the both of us) that my brother and I both fancied the same classmate, Arno Unruh. Arno was lean and gawky, with bird-like limbs, wore drooping corduroy pants and neatly pressed oxford shirts rolled up at the sleeves. His hair, sandy blond, seemed to aspire to straightness but lost its resolve and kinked on the ends. He had a friendly manner well-suited to his freckled, fair skin, and he was inclined equally toward chemistry and Unitarianism. His lips were eternally chapped, but behind Arno Unruh—those winsome good looks and ready sermons about selflessness and moral rectitude, how he'd segue easily into a discussion of unstable isotopes—he was an unwitting heartbreaker, "Bible-thumping lothario," to use Rhonda Obenchain's epithet for him. She could not fathom the attraction. I looked into Arno's watery eyes and I could see him puzzling over the logistics of my sister and me coordinating our

them he had very straight teeth and the faintest lisp. I found him thoroughly fetching and drew pictures in my notebook of the Möbius strip of our intestines linked in infinity. I asked Arno if he'd be my lab partner, which made my brother sulk, though he tried to look cheerful as he steadied the alembic for the alchemy of Rhonda Obenchain, school sorceress, his partner. Rhonda wore black clothing that occasionally shimmered and kohled circles around her eyes; an amulet fashioned of amber (which she claimed her great grandmother had smuggled from Poland, clutched tightly in her vagina as she dodged the penetrating stares of border dragoons) dangled around her neck, and the beat of my brother's heart grew faint in her presence. Though she referred to us as Frick and Frack or Chang and Eng, these were endearments coming from Rhonda, and I espied appetite in her smudged eyes when she batted them at my brother.

selflessness. My sister's XX-ray eyes burned through my jersey, through to my gnarled heart murmuring its ruined hunger.

Neither she nor I could be sure of the originating locus of our desire, but the skin below my navel pulsed and smoldered when I stole glances of Arno turning on the Bunsen burner, recording data in his college-ruled notebook. This, just when I thought I'd all but shed this shambly and unpredictable skin, bequeathing all its urges to my sister. I knew any hint of my being smitten would seem mutinous to her, so I balled up my fist and held it fast to my abdomen, willed my stomach to ache.

I pictured her years hence at a midtown ashram performing self-trepanation, drilling a hole in her skull that she imagined would lead her to the altar at which God Himself worshipped, the heart of the heart of divinity.

Arno made corny, clean jokes as we performed our experiments, and I imagined him in the basement of his church at a youth group social performing the same shtick, hair disheveled, lopsided grin, girls in long skirts and flat shoes smiling yearningly at him with each predictable punch line, dog-eared copies of the *Living Bible* clutched to their chests. I longed to corrupt him.

One day Rhonda, who it was clear found Arno insufferable, said, "How do you make a dead baby float?"

"That's disgusting," said Arno. Rhonda looked to my brother for counterpoint. I could have told her he would not look up from the scarred, black table.

"Two scoops of ice cream, root beer, and a dead baby,"

I could feel Rhonda Obenchain gazing at me sometimes across the table. When I finally dared to look up, I'd catch her licking her red, candied lips. She'd cock her head suggestively, reminding me of a famished wolverine that has stumbled upon a wayward lamb grazing obliviously, far from the flock. Watching *Wild Kingdom* every Sun-

she said, grinning, her braces glinting tauntingly. I could see she had practiced being spellbinding. At that moment, my brother straightened in his seat and glanced up at Arno, and I saw a meaningful look pass between them. There was a brief pause, then Arno shook his head, and my brother looked again at the table, slumped. Rhonda arched her eyebrows at me. I couldn't decode all of this swiftly enough to come to any satisfying conclusion and spent the rest of the class period trying not to think about it, staring at the periodic chart on the wall. I cursed 39, yttrium, Y, named for a town in Sweden, Ytterby, a cold place with Y's to spare, a melting point of 1523°C. I pictured my brother in a bubbling cauldron. He began to kick his feet.

Several experiments later, I confronted my brother about the knowing glances he kept shamelessly lobbing at Arno, and he said, in a tone that indicated he was

day night, I died a thousand deaths as those pronghorn deer, snowshoe rabbits, kangaroo rats misstepped and were snapped in the jaws or talons of cunning predators. I learned at a young age the futility of cheering on the defenseless, and I understood now that one false hop and I'd be helpless and wriggling in Rhonda's bangled clutches.

smiling smugly, though he wasn't, Benedict Cheshire Cat Arnold, double-agent quisling, "I am offspring of your rib. What did you expect?"

I had the lion's share of our internal apparatus, it was true, which was why we were eternally wedded, our intimacy inoperable, though *he'd* always had custody of the soul, docile lamb, bleating softly until the bequest of the earth was officially his, and this had seemed to me a reasonable division of labor. I'd sin, he'd feel penitent, each to her own vocation.

Later, when I noticed Arno's hand on my brother's knee under the lunch table, I felt suddenly and irreversibly annulled. My brother sat there innocently, unflinching, and I wondered when it was he had seceded, when he'd left me, expatriated, to form desires of his own. Perhaps, I wondered, my body throbbing with inviolate contours, it had been his appetites all along that had nudged us this way and that. Perhaps I had al-

When my sister sniffed the pheromones wafting in the air between Arno and me, I was filled with shame and regret but also, I confess, with a certain buried satisfaction that my body, heap of rusting scrap, creaky and reticent, might be stirred to impulses not entirely honorable.

ways been more spirit gusting
beneath the shared dermis.

When we were born it
was unclear how much of
the body my brother would
ever be able to claim and
he was termed "parasitic."
Though he has always been
subtle, he confounded all
prognostications, even my
own, by forging an undeni-
able shape for himself, and
talk of excision, as if he were
little more than an ingrown
toenail, ceased. It occurred to
me now that he'd been helms-
man all along. It was I who
had been indulged, spared. *He*
suffered *me*.

*   *   *

It is the winter we have always feared, bitter and wet.
We are no fans of intem-
perate weather, my brother
and I. There is never enough
warmth to go around when
temperatures dip below forty
degrees. The blood races from
limb to organ, trying to keep
up with the demand.

Outside, turkey buzzards
perch in the leafless trees,
looking like strange, black

fruit, oversized ornaments.
They blink their eyes at me,
small heads nestled in the
fluffed pillows of their backs.
I threw a ham bone out between the trees, but the buzzards, whom I've never known
to be dissuaded from such
effortless spoils by any sort of
inclement conditions, were
apparently too cold to stir,
and it strikes me, as I watch
the wind ruffle their black
feathers, that they are right
not to move. Eating is an ob-
solete gesture, their lethargy
seems to say, survival something we've evolved beyond.
Eating only keeps you going
for another day, holds you
at arm's length from God,
exactly where I've always
wanted to be, but my resolve
is thinning.

Rutherford B. Hayes, nineteenth president of the United
States, was referred to in the
press and by resentful parti-
sans as Rutherfraud because
he'd won a narrow and contested electoral majority but
had lost the popular vote,
and this is suddenly how I

feel: fraudulent, in command
only by way of biological fiat.
I managed to corral more cells
than my brother, more fleet
than he even in gestation, but
now I feel a revolution perco-
lating inside me, the funda-
mental goo of self quarrelling
with itself, a cellular upris-
ing, and I understand that
no matter what bone anyone
throws me, I will lay my head
on my brother's shoulder and
think, "It is too cold to stir."
I imagine cartoon vultures
falling dead from the trees,
tongues hanging out of the
sides of their beaks, XX for
eyes, other vultures, eyes wide
and clear—the black, empty
OO of a rifle muzzle—crowded round, comically picking at
the remains.

One morning as we were getting ready for school, my sister
touched my creamed chin
and said to me that there is
no such thing as the ordinary. "The more you look at
a common thing," she said,
"the more refined your understanding of it becomes and,
somehow, the less familiar

it seems—in knowing something intimately, you defamiliarize it, grant it its due complexity. But the converse is also true," she said dreamily, eyes blank as portals, seeming to teeter on the brink of understanding something essential. I bristled at the philosophical cant of her head. "The more you look at an uncommon thing," she said, looking at me, then at herself, in the mirror, "the more you see how common it is. You reduce it in such a way as to make it nearly universal."

Flummoxed by this sudden combination of depth of thought and attentiveness to my ablutions, I tried to defuse the solemnity of this moment, as well as that of the grimly garbed phalanx of future moments I saw marching toward us: "Philosophers must be querulous by nature," I feebly quipped. "Must be a sleepless lot."

She laid her head on my shoulder. Oh, no, no: levity and capitulation! I knew the jig was up.

*   *   *

My sister has stopped eating.
Like an irradiated tumor, she
is shrinking. That's how she
once would have thought of
me, but that's not how I think
of her. I think of her as ballast.
She has kept us from lifting
off, fleeing the planet, which
we'd have done long ago had I
once had my druthers. As the
ballast lessens, I have to curl
my toes in the carpeting, cling
to banisters, so as not to rise
and hover. I have no intention
of increasing our notoriety.

She will not let me feed
her, and she sags at my side,
like a raincoat draped over my
arm. As I watch her skin grow
slack, see bones emerge, feel
the border between us lose
its elasticity, I sense that it is,
after all, in the body that one
knows whatever one can claim
to know about God; redemption occurs, courageously, at
this site of pain and decay.
Where would the challenge
be otherwise? Would we be so
stirred, for millennia, would
we still be talking about it,
if it were only the *spirit* of
Christ whose wispy wrists and

billowing feet had been staked
to the cross? It's the thought
of torn tendon and cracking
bone that makes us swoon.

I find this optimistic and
try to prop my sister up with
the news. After the resurrection, Jesus couldn't eat cabbage without expelling gas,
I say. He wasn't recognizable
at first, even to disciples, appeared haggard, if beatific,
and a dark shimmer followed
him everywhere, the body
stuttering. His footprints
always left behind a sticky,
sweet residue, like honey,
a postscript of the proto-
plasm of survival. And when
he walked on water, he sank
down to his ankles, nearly lost
heart. It's no walk in the park
being incorruptible, I tell her.
Resurrection takes a toll. The
body changes, I say, touching
her cheek, but it's still necessary, if only to register the
shifty spirit! She grins at me
weakly, beyond revelation.

*   *   *

The wan changeling, my sister, erodes from girl to appendage to tumor, hurtling
in the direction of idea. "XX,

XX, XX!" I whisper fiercely
in her ear, the code meant
to gather and stitch her cells
together, shape her back into
girlchild.

But, even in deliquescence,
it is her will that presides. I
feel my heart shrinking with
her, puckering, growing green,
a forgotten potato. Another
tack: I plant a plaintive kiss
on her waxen lips. Y, I breathe
into her, Y you? I think this
will rouse her, and she does
lift her head. Outside, birds
drop from branches like black
bombs, swoop toward a gristly
salvation. I imagine the wafer
of my sister's body placed
on my tongue, imagine the
salty flavor of shared organ,
shared illness, disputed border, divided desire. My own
body tick-ticks, the pinging
of a heated engine tired of
idling, awakened, animates
the loosening spirit spread
thin between us.

Hallie Out of This World

I was born of an indiscretion. This is how my father tells it. One night he lost his head. He was all body. Hands, penis, stomach, butt. With no head. It rolled away and left him to grope, the headless horseman without the horse. It was a bowling ball in search of pins, a cantaloupe in search of mouths. When he finally found it again, it had a baby to think about, anchoring it to its neck.

My father says after I was born, my mother came to his parents' house. My father was home from college for the summer. He hadn't seen or heard from her since the night her hot, oniony breath wafted across the barren pedestal of his neck. This is how I tell it.

She carried me bundled in tea towels and handed me to him, saying, "I have things to do. You can't expect me to stay home with a baby all day. I'm a busy person." Then she walked away, and he called, "Wait, where can I reach you?" And she said, "You can't." He says he can still hear her clickety heels on the driveway.

I have often wondered if I somehow bear their lack of intent like a caul. If *accident* is written into my skin.

"What did she look like?" I ask my father. "Her face? What did you notice when you looked at her face?" "I don't know," he tells me. "It was dark."

In our building there is a blind man. I like the tap-tap of his cane against stairs and cement. I like the sound of someone finding his way. This man is thin and stooped and he wears an earring, a small silver hoop. Once I held the door for him and touched the hand that held the cane. I said, "I could help you do your dishes. I could balance your checkbook." I whispered to my shoulder, "You are one man I could love."

*   *   *

He stopped in the middle of the doorway and straightened up as best he could. His bent posture stemmed from a desire to know the terrain before he traversed it; as he walked he leaned forward to lengthen the sweep of his stick. He said, "I could eat you alive, little girl. Easy as any man." He grinned, exposing teeth that belonged in an American Dental Association commercial, the kind that would glint with magic sparkling stars punctuated by the ding of a bell. The glare of his teeth eclipsed his lips, his chin, his cheeks, his face. The world itself was swallowed up. All I could see were the steel points of his canines, the porcelain tiles of his two front teeth. Your teeth are blinding, I thought. I longed to be bitten.

Later he told me his name was Oedipus. Oed. His father's

sense of humor. "In my mind, I've killed him many times," Oed said.

I am Hallie, fifteen, and he is O-E-D, like the dictionary, twenty-eight.

Corky Roth is twelve and tall and smells like fallen leaves. He thinks he loves me. He lives in building D. I see him watching me from his living-room window. I see his mother pull the drapes on his adolescent yearning. On Valentine's Day this year, he gave me a card with a poem on it: *I like noodles, I like toast, I like bananas on my pot roast. I like peas, I like taters, I like chocolate on my tomaters! But, Valentine, I must confess, with a cherry on top I like you best!* On the card, a child balances on a large cherry and a halo of food floats above him the way cartoon bluebirds circle a steeple of smarting scalp.

It was better than the usual "Happy V.D." I said, "Robert Browning?"

He said, "What?" He said, "I could show you the place at Union Station where there are bullet holes from the Saint Valentine's Day Massacre, just like the big one in Chicago." His eyebrows were arched. He was waiting for me to say "Cool" or "Really?" or maybe "Get lost." I could see I was a wild card to him.

"Penis," I said, I don't know why. I liked the sound of it and had always wondered what it would feel like to say it aloud, out in the air, under the clouds, to see the breath it floated out on, to say it to a person who had one.

"Pardon?" he said. I smiled. Pardon. He broke my heart. On the bathroom wall of my mind, I crossed out the word I'd spoken and sniffed the Magic Marker instead. My father's head rolled by and winked.

*   *   *

I went to the animal genetics laboratory today. They won't allow me inside, of course. I stay outside where the animals take breaks from being experiments. I go there to visit Gretel. She is a cow too big for her legs. At the laboratory, they inject animals, farm animals mostly, with growth hormones that make them stretch and bulk to such proportions as only grade B horror movies can imagine. It is becoming a world that makes me feel small and wrong and out of place.

Gretel stands a good six-and-a-half feet when she is able. Her legs are not the kind of legs that can support her big brown girth for very long. I have never met legs in person that could, though sometimes on *Wild Kingdom* I see African elephants that make me envious on Gretel's behalf.

I am trying to strengthen Gretel. There is a small, grassy area where they sometimes let the cows roam, sit really. It's a small area, not that Oh-Give-Me-a-Home kind of place at all. I've uttered many a discouraging word there myself. I curse those shifty whitecoats. I've heard there are five-foot chickens whose eggs rival those of ostriches, though I have never seen one. The idea is omelettes and chicken chow mein for a family of forty, I guess, all from a single chicken. So Gretel gets to come out in the sun every day at noon, and I bring her things to eat, food that will make her strong and self-reliant. I am planning a breakout of sorts. Today I fed her lentil soup, an English muffin, cold oatmeal, and an apple, something for each of her stomachs. Neither of us cares for brussels sprouts.

Sometimes I read to her from the newspaper or tell her about current events on television. She sits close to the wooden fence and dips her head at an angle that allows a good scratch in the right spot. I told her about what I saw on the news last night. In a country called Bosnia, there are gray-haired children. A mother throws rocks at trucks filled with soldiers and shakes fists balled up like hard tumors. Her son was killed by her former neighbor, a man she had had to dinner many times, a man who ate carrots and leeks with her family. I can see his mouth chewing orange. There was a little girl in a hospital. Her legs below the knees had been bombed away. One minute she had legs and the next she was an image on television. As the camera passed her, she smiled. I don't think she knew what her lips were doing. Her mouth was shaping someone else's language. Like the pains she will feel in her airy shins, it was a phantom gesture.

I know a man who is a celebrity look-alike. He lives in building A. There is not much call for celebrity look-alikes in Kansas, but occasionally it is lucrative. His name is Preston, Preston Fryatt. He looks like Woody Allen, and he has developed a stuttering, hand-flailing banter that is very convincing, though a midwestern twang lurks beneath his vowels. Two years ago, the Tivoli Theater had a Woody Allen Film Festival, and they hired Preston to pace back and forth in the lobby and recite from Woody's movies and stand-up routines, monologues about sex and death and Kierkegaard. Afterward, Preston said, "You know, the sources of angst are increasing." He told me that when he was younger he looked a little like Wally Cox, the voice of Underdog. He says he has always had a face that makes people thumb through their pasts, searching mental mug shots for a match. If people do not identify him as Woody Allen, they often look at him with narrow eyes, then say, "Weren't you once my tax attorney?" or "Didn't I see you on *America's Most Wanted*?" Since Woody's marital tribulations, Preston has had to be wary of the public. Woody's backers are kind but reproachful; they approach him and say things like, "I never knew what you saw in that Mia Ferret, anyway. Didn't you see *Rose Marie's Baby*? You should have been forewarned." The supporters of Mia he encounters at grocery stores sometimes become violent, clubbing him with baguettes or produce. Preston never leaves his house without his ascot and a hat tipped over his eyes. He waits for the storm to pass.

Oed and I are friends now. I could see it in his teeth that he would never eat me alive. He is angry, yes, and beautiful. I love the nothing that his eyes are, saucers of speckled milk. I love the nothing that I am in front of them. Oed hates it when I talk this way. He says I romanticize misfortune, that I am an annoying bleeding heart who has the luxury to be one. He says I seize on the shortcomings, disabilities, grief, and misery of others out of a sense of guilt over my own gentle and easy life. He calls it emotional sleight-of-hand. He is not as well acquainted with my heart as he thinks he is. I piss him off less than I used to.

Last year I met a man living, temporarily, next door to Preston. He was a college professor visiting for a semester. He had written a book and he told me things. He came here from Germany, but he had lived in Alaska, Australia, Mexico, even Siberia. He knew about the religious practices of many tribal cultures and he told me stories. One night he said, "Your skin gives off light. I'm going to teach you to dream." He said in all cultures there are gods and goddesses and spirits who watch over us, look inside us, see who we really are, help us to find special strength. He told me about a medicine man he knew in Australia. When this man was still a novice, he went to a cave where the spirits of his ancestors lived. He carried with him his grandmother's head scarf. He slept deep in the cave and dreamed until the spirits came to him. They put their billowing hands inside him and pulled out all his organs, his liver, his kidneys, his lungs and his heart. They scooped out his brain and unhinged his penis. They snapped his eyes out and held them in the dark mist of their floating fingers. His eyes rolled around and looked at the world. Then these ancestral wraiths plugged in new ones, new parts that would help him to heal other people, heal himself. And they slipped in extras, little crystal eggs that would expand and glow, aid him in mending broken souls. Then the man began to float and he lilted out of the cave on waves of air. He flew up and clung to the sky. The medicine man left this world and when he came back, he knew how to navigate pain. It took all of time to do this.

"Go and dream, Hallie," the professor said. "Fly."

I recently tried my hand at love connecting. I am o for one. It's not as easy as it looks on television. I thought I had a sure-shot match. Willette Mertz lives in building C. Hierarchically speaking, building C is the one we all strive for. If this apartment complex were karma, building C would be nirvana. All the apartments come with fireplaces, microwave ovens, miniblinds, and walk-in closets you could easily store several recreational vehicles in, and in the basement there are two laundry rooms kept so clean you could probably have an emergency appendectomy on the folding table without risking infection. One room even has a bill changer and Coke machine. It's cush. I thought the fact Willette lives in C would automatically give her a status edge. I told Preston he should meet her. "Maybe you could do your laundry together," I said. I hoped I might be invited.

Willette is a fiend for the color pink. Though Preston denies it, I think it is this fact that sounded the death knell to the potential blossoming of romance, this and Willette's tight lips regarding Preston's fate. When you first walk into Willette's apartment, it's as though you've stepped inside a well-lit mouth: pink overhead, to the sides, and underfoot. It's disorienting. The first time I entered Willette's apartment, my intestines began to vibrate. I had to leave. But I kept going back and stayed longer and longer each time. Now I am acclimated and hours pass before I get woozy.

Willette had to lobby the management to exchange the muted and innocuous color scheme for one most often seen covering the lips and fingernails of dressy women. She paid for the transformation herself and she has to pay to have it returned to its origins of white and gray when she leaves. Willette earns a good living selling Mary Kay Cosmetics and reading palms on the side.

(People in these parts are very skittish about colors that slap them awake, colors that compete instead of conform. We live in a community in which the presence of a White Castle hamburger stand was hotly contested because it was to be built in the parking lot of Loehmann's Plaza, whose uniformity of beige exteriors had been strictly dictated by city council. The White Castle people did not want to be beige. The council people said if they did it for one community, suddenly you'd see Green Castles and Blue Castles and possibly even Puce Castles popping up all over the place. Complete anarchy. White Castle would come to mean nothing, half-baked, impetuous notions. They couldn't have that. The debate raged for months—the White Castle people as unbudgeable as the beige-committed community—until one night my father stood up at a council meeting and screamed, "It's a goddamned White Castle for Christ's sake! They serve hamburgers that fit three to a mouth. Who gives a rat's ass?" My father was asked to leave, but it was too late, the seeds of dissent had been sown. The White Castle now looms pleasantly out of place, like Lincoln Logs among Legos, in the parking lot of Loehmann's Plaza.)

Willette and I went to this White Castle for chocolate shakes and she cheered "Hoo-hoo!" when I told her the story behind it. It was this that gave me the Cupid bug in the first place. She said she loved underdogs. I knew she must meet Preston.

Before we went over to Willette's, Preston was nervous and mumbling, searching for an identity he could call his own. He said, "Hallie, I don't know who I am anymore."

I said, "You're Preston Fryatt, and don't you forget it."

"I'm Preston Fryatt, I'm Preston Fryatt, Preston Fryatt," he whispered solemnly, as if he were chanting a life-or-death phone number on the way to a distant pay phone.

Then he stopped and looked at me with small, dark eyes behind thick lenses, floating like tiny fish in an aquarium. "But what does that mean? What do I think about national health care?" he said. "Or petting zoos or the sight of blood?"

"For, no comment, against," I said. Preston's forehead became crimped. "Preston, relax. Willette's easygoing. She won't press you for particulars on the first meeting."

Preston stared down at his penniless loafers. "I haven't had a date in two years," he said. "I don't even know if the, you know," he began to whisper, *"e-q-u-i-p-m-e-n-t* still works."

Preston and I often watched television together on Sunday nights and I knew from his viewing habits he had come to see sex as something to forestall extinction. "Preston," I said, "you've been watching too many wildlife programs. This isn't about mating. The propagation of the species does not depend on this meeting. You're just going to make the acquaintance of one of your neighbors."

Preston nodded and looked up, the fish of his eyes now floating near the top of the tank.

As Preston entered Willette's apartment, he walked slowly and held his hands out to his sides as if to steady himself. I guided him to the rose-print couch and sat him down. The pupils of his eyes seemed to shrink and dilate like breathing. Willette's apartment affected Preston in the manner of a pocket watch on a shiny gold chain that swings to the lilt of a voice, calming as a foot rub, chanting *sleepy, sleepy.*

"You look familiar to me, Preston," Willette, of course, said. She sat in a rocking chair opposite him and stared and nodded. "Have you ever been married? Maybe I sold your wife some cosmetics?"

"I've never been married," Preston said. The way Preston spoke, without inflection, made it sound as though he'd been programmed. I thought of *2001: A Space Odyssey,* that movie with the fetus bobbing in the ether. Preston brought to mind the diabolical computer Hal 9000, although he was currently exhibiting less personality and no apparent chess skills. I hoped Willette was not making this same association. I sensed my yet-to-be-earned reputation as a shrewd matchmaker was in jeopardy. I casually kicked Preston in the calf. "You?" Preston asked, although it sounded sort of accusatory, like the kind of *you* that follows a *hey*.

"Yes," Willette said. "Technically, I guess I still am."

"You're married?" Preston asked. He looked at me as he said this. I could tell he was thinking about all the trouble he'd gone through scrambling for a self and fretting about his equipment and all.

Willette said, "Joseph and I haven't seen one another in over five years, so I figure we've got us a common-law divorce." Willette began to rock. "Joseph's best feature was his toes. You'd never expect a man so strapping to have such lovely feet, but his toes were hairless and white, flat and squared off at the nails like piano keys. I swear I nearly swooned the first time I saw them.

"But, well, you know." Willette stopped rocking; she straightened her legs out in front of her and wiggled her feet. "Toes in and of themselves do not a marriage make. When Joseph was in a state, which was common enough, he'd go out in the streets and look for cats to kick. So whenever we had a fight, I had to race out of the house and run up and down the streets clanging a ladle against a kettle until all the animals were safely spooked."

"Wow," I said.

"Yep." Willette sat forward. "Say, Preston, has anyone ever read your palm?"

Preston shook his head and looked down at his hands. "Um, my mother used to check the bumps on my head to see if I, I, I would be going to medical school, but, you know, hands, I, no." Woody was slipping in.

"Are you a religious man, Preston?" Willette moved over to the couch and squeezed between Preston and me.

"Well, I mean, sure, unless, you know, there's something better on television." I shot Preston a look equivalent to a sock in the arm. As Willette took Preston's hand in hers, I moved over to the rocking chair. She rubbed her thumb over his palm and Preston began to smile.

"Do you have experience at this?" he asked.

"Mm-hmm. It was one of the things that made Joseph apoplectic, the fact that I could see in the notched lines on his hands the hardships he had yet to negotiate. This riled him fierce. 'Let me tell *you* something,' he'd say. 'I predict a knuckle sandwich in your future,' then he'd raise his fist in front of his face, 'so if you don't want to add this to your diet, I suggest you abandon this crackpot visionary babbling of yours. My fate is not in your hands.' And I'd say, 'No, but it's in yours.'" Willette held her finger on a line as though she were pointing to something on a map. "Says here you're likely to have quite a brood, Preston, and . . ." Willette stopped and squinted, then her eyes got big and she raised her head up. She dropped Preston's hand and said, "Oh, my stars!" She looked at me. She looked at Preston.

"What?" Preston asked. "What is it?" Willette patted Preston's shoulder. "Anyone for a cheese puff?" She stood up quickly and sailed into her pearly pink kitchen.

And that was it. I could not imagine what sinister thing it was Willette espied in the creases of Preston's telling palm, but it was enough for her to force an hors d'oeuvre and cold beverage on us in a hurry, then after a bite and sip beg off with a forgotten appointment. Willette sealed her lips and shook her head. When she finally spoke, all she said as she worried a twist of hair and swept us out of her apartment, whose now pulsating pink interior seemed on the verge of a swallow, was that "the responsibility of deciphering the dialect of hands" had grown "too weighty." She said, "I am aiming my energies at peddling blush and concealer, things that hide and blind those old loud-mouthed lines."

Eventually Willette spilled it. Though I had to promise to breathe nary a syllable to Preston ("Sometimes these things can be overcome, it's written in flesh not stone, but sometimes aware-ness of a possibly foreboding fate can be feared so much it's self-fulfilling"), Willette divulged some visionary details. She said that after years of being kind and quiet and humble and awkward, Preston would one day see dreams hoped for in dark silence come screaming into the light of day. "He'll have the world by the tail. He'll swing it round and round with nothing left to lasso. We're talking the Big Payload, El Grande Oyster, and all that hoopla." She said one day he'd have fame and fortune, peace and new love.

I could feel my brows knitting. I said, "Cut to it, Willette. One day Preston will have it all. And . . . ?"

She said, "And that's just it. It lasts *one day*. On the same day he reaches his zenith, he dies a random death. He steps in front of something, a deadly virus, a bus, a bullet, a woman scorned, I don't know what. I just know it all ends the minute he breathes easy."

"Yipes," I said. I didn't care a bit for the notion that the cosmos had a wicked sense of irony. Willette nodded, her face pinched in chagrin.

I told Oed about it and he told me all my friends were flakes. "You're my friend," I said.

Oed aimed his face at my voice. His lips were reddish and wet, juicy, arrogant plums. "Come here," he said.

I moved from the beanbag chair to the couch. He took my hand. I jerked, but he gripped it firmly. He ran his fingers over my palm. I imagined my body as a tablet of Braille, bumps and lines he could read, decode. He could tell me who I am. I almost wet my pants. I have to keep my head on my neck, I thought.

"What's this?" he asked. He traced the scar across my palm. I jerked again. His grip tightened.

"It's mine," I said.

"Hmm. Tender?" He held my hand in front of his eyes, my wrist a handle, angled up, as if my palm were a magnifying glass through which he might see the ceiling, the sky, the world beyond his dead view. He touched the scar again. "The ridge of fate," he said. He smiled. His sunny teeth flashed. "You will live in infamy," he said. "You're a fast burning centrifuge spinning spirit from flesh." Oed winked, the slow lowering of a perfunctory eyelid, a sighted gesture I had taught him. I told him it meant *Between you and me, I know who you really are.* "You don't get fortunes like that from a cookie," he said. He dropped my hand and grinned. "Get me some socks, Hal."

When I handed him the socks, he felt them and smelled them and said, "These are mismatched." It was true: one black, one green. Oed had a strongly developed tactile sense of color that I was always trying to trump.

*   *   *

Oedipus builds violins and I watch. I love to see him feel his way through the wood; the maple, the spruce lure his fingers to just the right place and he sculpts with such loving delicacy, I imagine the ghost of Stradivari ecstatically swirling through a seizure of clouds. I love to hear Oed talk as he works, naming the parts for me: pegbox and purfling and f-hole and bass bar, neck, ribs and belly, my own crackling beneath the words, the resonant body he molds.

It is on one of these nights as I watch him rub and shape, pull contours from wood, that I decide to undress. I take off my shoes and socks, jeans and underpants, shirt and bra and lay them on the couch. As I do this, I wait for the moment when he will hear the eager rustle of fabric and ask what I am doing. But he doesn't. So I move to him, slowly. I don't want him to notice the sound of my flesh moving against itself. I bend over his back curved with purpose and put my lips to his neck. He stiffens, stops breathing. I place my hands over his eyes. "Guess who?" I say. I bend farther and place my cheek against his hot neck.

"Hallie," he says. He sets his work down and turns in his chair. "Don't."

I hold his face in my hands. I kneel and smile up into his emptied eyes. "What do you see?"

He takes my hands by the wrists. "Goddamn it, Hallie," he whispers. "I'm blind, but that doesn't mean I can teach you anything. I can't fucking sensitize you to the world. I can't help you see things that aren't there. I'm not a prophet, I'm not a poet. I'm a goddamn blind man, and I eat and shit and build violins, so leave me the fuck alone."

I stand up and lean forward, press my breast to his parted lips.

*   *   *

When I was eight years old, I heard a sound like a low scream and I walked toward it. I was visiting my grandparents, who lived in a neighborhood with farms. The sound came from a nearby clearing. When I got to the field, I saw a cow walking slowly back and forth, as though she couldn't remember where she lived. And then I saw a naked man, my first, and I froze. The naked man's hair was frizzed and spoked out in all directions like flames. He had blood on his hands and chest, and he looked and looked at me. He raised his hands above his head, as though I were going to take him prisoner. I walked backward until my feet hit the gravel, then I turned and ran.

The next time I saw a naked man, I was walking home from school, crossing Pierson Park. A man in a three-piece suit and hat appeared next to me in the quiet air. He elbowed me, showed me a black-handled knife. He pointed his head in the direction of a stand of trees. I looked into his gray eyes, the color of something tarnished. His blond hair was slicked back and I could smell his cologne. We walked until a dense thickness of trees surrounded us. He told me to take off my clothes and he also began to undress. My legs ached and trembled; it felt as though I'd just crossed a continent, entered a foreign land. I tried to stiffen them. I didn't want him to see me shake.

When we were both naked, I stared at his penis. It looked like an egg hidden in bleached grass. The naked man smiled. I smiled back. His grin straightened and he said, "Shut up."

He laid the knife down in the grass and held his hands up in front of him. His hands were smallish and clean, his palms unremarkable. He said, "I won't hurt you." He said, "Some of us just say that, but I really mean it." He came closer to me and got on his knees. I stood still with my hands at my sides, licking my lips over and over again. I had this impulse to pat him on the head, touch his cheeks, but I was afraid my hands might choose a path of their own, might hook their fingers into his eyes.

"I just want to look," he said. He raised his hands between us and held them in front of my chest; they hovered in front of the humble beginnings of breasts. I leaned backward and he shook his finger at me. Then he began moving his hands up and down, around, miming desire; he never touched me. It was as though a plate of glass separated us, glass he pretended was hot skin. Then he put his hands down and just looked.

I tried hard to think of escape and survival but strange things darted into my thoughts and edged out my instincts, my panic. An image flashed in my mind: my father's jeweled cuff links that I so loved to hide under my covers, pretending they were magic eyes that could see me in the dark. I remembered the bus I had passed earlier. It was a white school bus with a red hood and two stripes that ran the length of it. Red letters on one side announced: C H _ _ C H. *What's Missing?* U R! I thought of God. I thought of how they say God sees everything, every single thing, even things far inside us, like bad thoughts and broken bones. I thought of God, thought he's watching me now, careful to keep quiet, watching and watching. I looked at the man. I wanted to polish his eyes. I breathed.

He moved his face close to my body but didn't touch. His eyes moved across my skin, and I felt the sticky legs of beetles inching along my chest and throat and stomach and thighs. My body itched. His eyes circled the dots of my nipples, traveled around my navel, migrating along the bare V between my legs. I wondered if God saw me now, if there was a me to see.

My hand reached out for the man's shoulder and he fell backward with a quick inhalation of air. "Touch me," I said. "Touch!" He shook his head and put his hands to his mouth. I cupped my small breast. He put his hands in front of his face and shook his head. "Look at me!" I yelled. The shaking in my legs moved up through the rest of my body and I lunged into the grass and groped for the knife. The naked man sat on his knees and buried his face in his hands. "Look," I said, holding the knife. I ran the blade across my palm. I felt the knife cut, but it wasn't what I expected to feel. It felt like it was an opening that had been there all along. The naked man shook his head and cried into his fingers.

Each time I play this memory back in my head, I change what I felt during the ten minutes it took for this to happen. Sometimes I make myself feel terror or shame or horror or anger so hot it burns the inside of my head to conjure it; sometimes I even feel longing. And when I think about it now, I feel all of those things. But I realize what I felt then, when it was over, was envy. I know this is not the right thing to feel, but I felt it. I envied his power to decide to spend ten minutes changing a little girl's life.

*   *   *

Oed pushes me back by the shoulders and lowers his head. "Hallie, don't do this. I can't . . ."

I say, "There was a man. He was naked. I was twelve." Oed raises his head. His blown-out eyes twitch back and forth. I sit on his lap. He hugs me to him and rocks. I touch his cheek. "What do you see?" I ask.

"Nothing." He closes his eyes. I touch his eyelid. I feel his sightless eye, an excess like the wings of penguins, flutter beneath my finger. He sits me up and steadies my face in front of his. "Hallie," he says.

I cross my arms and grip my shoulders. I squeeze my arms, my thighs, my hands. My skin is warm.

*   *   *

Yesterday I went to the animal lab to visit Gretel again. I fed her popcorn and carrots and told her about the massacre in Hebron. A man walked into the mosque in the Tomb of the Patriarchs. He had a machine gun. He opened fire on praying people. The shooting lasted six or seven minutes. He killed men and boys. Thirty or maybe more. Survivors jumped the gunman and beat him to death. A five-year-old boy was shot in the back of the leg. His father, an ambulance driver, arrived on the scene and saw his son, bleeding, cradled in the arms of his uncle. The boy lived.

Gretel's sticky lips and tongue pumped and slid. The slimy velveteen space between her nostrils bobbed. Strings of sleepy wetness oozed from her eyes. A young man in a white lab coat paced nearby. When I first arrived, he told me Gretel's bones were beginning to give, that she was growing less and less able to stand on her own. He told me he was not the one who thought this up, this experiment was not his idea. "I'm just an intern," he said. He told me he loved animals, that he had a dog and a canary and a salamander at home. I watched his eyes stare at Gretel. "What do you see?" I asked.

It is late at night and I have been sleeping. My window is open and in the breath of wind that stirs through my room I can smell that it has rained. The light from the moon spills onto my futon and washes across my bare feet. I sit up. I rummage under my bed frame and pull out a box. I open the lid. Underneath photographs and envelopes filled with baby teeth and fine curls of hair lie the two tea towels I once wore. I pull them out and carry them with me, walk outside.

As I stand in front of my building, I hear someone walking on the sidewalk. I see black sling-back pumps clicking toward me. A woman with my face approaches, her arms open. She stops in front of me and smiles. Taking my hand, she leads me to the area between buildings. I blink and blink and see people in the moonlit grass. They are sitting around a cow, my Gretel. A little girl whose legs stop at the knees links hands with a boy with a bandaged thigh. Oed is there, and he holds a violin and waves at me with the bow. The woman leads me into the circle and I see the skin on my arms begin to flash, a neon stutter. I drop the towels. Oed stands and Gretel unfolds her brittle legs, shaky bamboo stalks, and wobbles upward. The boy rises, hoists the girl in his arms. Oed begins to run the bow across the strings of the violin and as it hums, Gretel and Oed and I lift into the air. We lift up and up, floating over buildings and trees, looping through power lines, listing near towers ablink in the night, and I feel my heart swivel inside me; my lungs bubble and fizz. I hold onto Gretel's neck as she paddles the breeze, her gentle lowing rumbling beneath my hand. Oed clutches my waist, sandwiching me between fiddle and bow; we are music in the making. And as we float higher and higher into the ionized air, far from all that's familiar and heavy, I know we'll continue to weave through the atmosphere and scale the sky until the bottoms of our superlunar hooves and feet, all that is visible from earth, flash a spectral exit, and then we will sizzle, devoured by scalding stars, and burn ourselves out of this world.

The Flannery O'Connor Award for Short Fiction

T. M. McNally, *Low Flying Aircraft*

Alfred DePew, *The Melancholy of Departure*

Dennis Hathaway, *The Consequences of Desire*

Rita Ciresi, *Mother Rocket*

Dianne Nelson, *A Brief History of Male Nudes in America*

Christopher McIlroy, *All My Relations*

Alyce Miller, *The Nature of Longing*

Carol Lee Lorenzo, *Nervous Dancer*

C. M. Mayo, *Sky over El Nido*

Wendy Brenner, *Large Animals in Everyday Life*

Paul Rawlins, *No Lie Like Love*

Harvey Grossinger, *The Quarry*

Ha Jin, *Under the Red Flag*

Andy Plattner, *Winter Money*

Frank Soos, *Unified Field Theory*

Mary Clyde, *Survival Rates*

Hester Kaplan, *The Edge of Marriage*

Darrell Spencer, *CAUTION Men in Trees*

Robert Anderson, *Ice Age*

Bill Roorbach, *Big Bend*

Dana Johnson, *Break Any Woman Down*

Gina Ochsner, *The Necessary Grace to Fall*

Kellie Wells, *Compression Scars*